THE SHADOW ON THE WALL

Books by Ruskin Bond

Fiction

Miracle at Happy Bazaar: My Very Best Stories for Children
Rhododendrons in the Mist: My Favourite Tales of the Himalaya
A Gallery of Rascals: My Favourite Tales of Rogues, Rapscallions and Ne'er-do-wells
Unhurried Tales: My Favourite Novellas
Small Towns, Big Stories
Upon an Old Wall Dreaming
A Gathering of Friends
Tales of Fosterganj
The Room on the Roof & Vagrants in the Valley
The Night Train at Deoli and Other Stories
Time Stops at Shamli and Other Stories
Our Trees Still Grow in Dehra
A Season of Ghosts
When Darkness Falls and Other Stories
A Flight of Pigeons
Delhi Is Not Far
A Face in the Dark and Other Hauntings
The Sensualist
A Handful of Nuts
Maharani
Secrets

Non-fiction

It's a Wonderful Life: Roads to Happiness
Rain in the Mountains
Scenes from a Writer's Life
Landour Days
Notes from a Small Room
The India I Love

Anthologies

A Town Called Dehra
Classic Ruskin Bond: Complete and Unabridged
Classic Ruskin Bond Volume 2: The Memoirs
Dust on the Mountain: Collected Stories
Friends in Small Places
Ghost Stories from the Raj
Great Stories for Children
Tales of the Open Road
The Essential Collection for Young Readers
Ruskin Bond's Book of Nature
Ruskin Bond's Book of Humour
The Writer on the Hill

Poetry

Hip-Hop Nature Boy & Other Poems
Ruskin Bond's Book of Verse

THE SHADOW ON THE WALL

My Favourite Stories
of Ghosts, Spirits,
and Things that Go Bump in the Night

Ruskin Bond

ALEPH BOOK COMPANY
An independent publishing firm
promoted by *Rupa Publications India*

First published in India in 2021
by Aleph Book Company
7/16 Ansari Road, Daryaganj
New Delhi 110 002

Copyright © Ruskin Bond 2021

All previously published text material in the
book has appeared in books published by Rupa
Publications India and Aleph Book Company and has
been used with the permission of the publishers and
the author.

All rights reserved.

The author has asserted his moral rights.

This is a work of fiction. Names, characters,
places, and incidents are either the product of the
author's imagination or are used fictitiously and any
resemblance to any actual persons, living or dead,
events or locales is entirely coincidental.

No part of this publication may be reproduced,
transmitted, or stored in a retrieval system, in any
form or by any means, without permission in writing
from Aleph Book Company.

ISBN: 978-93-90652-78-5

3 5 7 9 10 8 6 4

Printed in India

This book is sold subject to the condition that it
shall not, by way of trade or otherwise, be lent,
resold, hired out, or otherwise circulated without the
publisher's prior consent in any form of binding or
cover other than that in which it is published.

CONTENTS

Introduction vii

1. The Shadow on the Wall 1
2. The Overcoat 10
3. The Skull 15
4. Fairy Glen Palace 24
5. Eyes of the Cat 38
6. Susanna's Seven Husbands 42
7. Whispering in the Dark 50
8. The Chakrata Cat 58
9. A Face in the Dark 63
10. Ghost Trouble 66

11. The Doppelgänger	83
12. The Wind on Haunted Hill	90
13. Welcome, Good Spirits!	98
14. The Whistling Schoolboy	101
15. Some Hill Station Ghosts	109
16. The Man Who Was Kipling	120
17. The Ghost and the Idiot	126
18. The Trouble with Jinns	132
19. Wilson's Bridge	139
20. A Face Under the Pillow	147
21. Haunted Places	151

INTRODUCTION

We have all been housebound for the better part of two years, and those of us who are, by nature, bookish people, have probably suffered less from this enforced isolation than most people. I have read more, written more, and consumed more mangoes than at any other time in my life.

A kind reader kept sending me mangoes, lovely sweet juicy ones. Another sent me a set of Wordsworth reprints devoted to supernatural fiction of the nineteenth century. I wallowed in the ghost stories of M. R. James, Edith Wharton, Oliver Onions (that was his real name), and others who had been rescued from oblivion—Henry S. Whitehead with his *Voodoo Tales* from the West Indies, and Mrs J. H. Riddell's whimsical Irish ghost stories called *Night Shivers*. And some of their weird tales really did give me the shivers.

Talking of oblivion, the first ghost story that I wrote, back in 1956 or '57, has also vanished like a forgotten ghost. It was called 'Have You Ever Been in Love With a Ghost?' and it appeared in *the Illustrated Weekly of India*, then edited by a genial Irishman called C. R. Mandy, who published many of my early stories before retiring to a tiny island off the coast of Sri Lanka. I have long since lost my carbon copy of the typescript (no photocopiers in those far-off days), and if the story still exists it will be found in the archives of that venerable magazine, hopefully preserved in the files of the Times of India group.

It doesn't really matter. I have written bundles of ghost stories since then, and a number of vintage tales appear in this selection, along with a few that were written during the recent pandemic.

One of my early stories, 'A Face in the Dark', recently found its way into the school curriculum, and some students have written to me saying they were puzzled by the story's inconclusive ending. 'And what happened then?' they want to know. What happened to Mr Oliver after he had seen the boy without a face, followed by the featureless chowkidar?

Well, when I first wrote this story the last line read: 'And that was when Mr Oliver had his heart attack.' But

Introduction

later I felt sorry for Mr Oliver, a lonely bachelor who taught us geography, so I deleted that final sentence and saved him from a heart attack.

But in order to please those who would like a more conclusive ending to the story, I hereby give it another twist:

> Mr Oliver, frightened out of his wits, dashed across the playing field to his rooms. He made straight for the mirror on his dressing table, expecting to see a reflection of his own blank featureless face. But there was nothing to be seen. No reflection, nothing at all. He had gone digital.

Will that do?

Or, will there be another chorus of 'What happened next?'

What will happen next—to all of us, to the world at large? Perhaps, like the astrologers, we must consult the stars. Or the ghosts of aeons yet to come.

Ruskin Bond
Landour
June 2021

THE SHADOW ON THE WALL

When I was in my early twenties, a struggling freelance writer, I rented two small rooms above a shop in Dehradun, and settled down to make my fortune as an author. Or so I hoped.

The rooms were without electricity, the landlord (the shop owner) having failed to pay the electricity bills for several years; but this did not bother me. Dehra wasn't too hot in those days, and I had no need of a ceiling fan. And I thought an oil lamp would be sufficient and even quite romantic. Hadn't the great authors of the past penned their masterpieces by the light of a solitary lamp? I could picture Goethe labouring over his *Faust*, Shakespeare over his *Sonnets*, Dostoyevsky over his *Crime and Punishment* (probably in a prison cell) and Emily Brontë composing

Wuthering Heights by the light of a flickering lamp while a snowstorm raged across the moors that surrounded her father's lonely parsonage.

Many geniuses would have written by lamplight—Premchand in his village, Keats in his attic, poor John Clare in a madhouse.... Well, I was no genius and I had no wish to enter a madhouse, but I liked the idea of writing by lamplight, so I invested in a lamp and a bottle of kerosene, set up the lamp on an old dining table (I took my meals at a dhaba down the road), brought it to a fine glow, and wrote a new story under its benediction.

I don't remember what the story was about, but it wasn't a bad effort, and I sold it to a Sunday magazine.

Every evening, after taking my meal in the dhaba, I would light the lamp, settle down at the table, and toss off a story or an article. I enjoyed the lamplight, even when I wasn't writing. There was something soothing about its soft glow. It threw my shadow on the wall on the other side of the desk; and whenever I got up and paced about the room (as I often do when writing) my shadow would follow, prowling about on the walls of the room, almost as though it were taking on a life of its own.

The shadow was always a little larger than life. The lamp seemed to magnify my image. Probably this had something to do with the glass or the position of the lamp. And late one evening, while I was in the middle of a story, I chanced to look up—and there, beside my shadow on the wall, was another shadow. It was the shadow of someone who was standing behind me.

Someone was in the room, looking over my shoulder, reading what I was writing.

It is always irritating to have someone watching you while you work. Even in an exam hall I could never proceed with my essay or answers if the supervisor was standing over me; I would wait for him to move on, so that I could concentrate properly.

So now, disturbed, I turned around to see who was looking over my shoulder.

There was no one behind me, no one was in the room.

I can't say I was frightened. But I felt extremely uneasy. Had I imagined the shadow on the wall—the shadow of the watcher? I looked again. It was no longer there.

I returned to my writing. But I was uneasy. I couldn't help feeling that I was not alone, that someone was reading my manuscript even as it was being written.

Well, doesn't every writer cherish a reader? Why complain? If there can be ghostwriters there can be ghost readers.

And when I looked up again the shadow was there, standing beside my own seated shadow, very still, studying

The Shadow on the Wall

the page, my words, my stream of consciousness.

It was the shadow of a woman, of that I was certain. Her hair fell to her shoulders, the outline of her figure was feminine, and she was wearing a gown that trailed behind her. All this the shadow told me; but no more.

I put down my pen, covered my manuscript with a paperweight, put out the lamp, and went to bed. In the dark there are no shadows.

∽

The dark has never really bothered me. With my poor sight I am just as home in the dark as I am in a well-lit room. That's why I like the lamplight. It is not too harsh, too intrusive; and beyond its circle of light, there is darkness, the friendly dark that is home to little bats, timid mice, and shy humans.

But lamps throw shadows. And when I sat down at my desk the following evening, I was expecting the shadow of my solitary reader.

I had written a page or two before I became aware of her presence. I knew she was there without looking up to see if her shadow was there on the wall. The room had become suffused with an unmistakable fragrance—attar of roses! She was speaking to me through the perfumes of her favourite flower.

But I was not to be seduced!

I carried on with my story—'Time Stops at Shamli'—completed a few pages, covered them up, put out the lamp, and went to bed.

My visitor must have been annoyed, because the scent of roses vanished, to be replaced by the strong odour of crushed marigolds. I covered my head with a blanket and shut out all scents and shadows.

Next morning I found the pages of my manuscript scattered about the floor of my room. Perhaps the dawn wind had disturbed them. The window was half open. Could my visitor have disturbed them? She was doing her best to make her presence known.

I started working in the mornings instead of at night. The lamp would be given a rest except when really needed. Let the shadows rest. Let the phantom lady rest....

She did not like being ignored.

Late one night—it must have been about two in the morning, the witches' hour—I was awakened by the most terrible shrieks. The room vibrated with the sounds of a shrieking woman.

Scared out of my wits, I leapt out of bed and lit the lamp, which now stood on the dressing table. The shrieking stopped. And shadows scurried about on the walls.

The Shadow on the Wall

This happened night after night, for almost a week. Shrieks would wake me in the middle of the night, and would stop only when the lamp was lit. No longer did fragrance fill the air; just the smell of oil and something burning.

I confided in Melaram, the owner of the dhaba where I took my meals. He twirled his luxurious moustache, nodded sagely, and said: 'It seems your landlord kept something from you—the tragedy of the woman who perished in your flat some five or six years ago. They were a childless couple, she and her doctor husband. They quarrelled a lot. One day, when she was in the kitchen preparing their dinner, the petromax stove burst, burning oil fell on her clothes and soon she was covered in flames. She ran on to the balcony, screaming for help, but by the time we could get to her she was in a terrible state.'

'And where was her husband?'

'Out, visiting a patient. He followed us to the hospital, but by then she had gone. In fact, there wasn't much left of her.'

'So it was an accident?'

'The police called it an accident. But there were rumours—there are always rumours in such cases, and when the doctor left town and set up his practice in

Delhi, there were more rumours. And then of course he married again....'

'All speculation,' I said, 'But I've had enough of the lady's presence. Her shadow seems real enough—and now those shrieks! I'm moving into the station hotel, and then perhaps you can help me find another flat.'

But I could not move immediately. Two suitcases held all my clothes and personal effects, but I had accumulated a cupboard full of books, and these, along with my notebooks and manuscripts, had to be carefully packed. It meant another night in my haunted rooms.

I went to bed as late as possible. I went to bed in the dark. Well, it wasn't too dark, because a full moon threw its beams across the balcony. But I did not light the lamp; I'd had enough of shadows.

I had asked Melaram's young assistant to bring me a glass of hot tea at daybreak. I slept soundly. There was no shrieking that night. But I was awakened by a push on my left shoulder. And I started up and called out 'What's up? Why so early?' thinking it was the boy with my tea. The moonlight had gone and it was dark everywhere.

I got no answer. Instead I received another push.

This annoyed me and I said, 'Why don't you speak, boy? Is something wrong?'

Still no answer, and as I began to sit up I felt a human

hand, warm, plump and soft, slip into mine.

Still thinking it was the boy, I held the hand; but my free hand encountered a wrist and arm, a long sleeveless arm. I felt along the arm, but when I reached the elbow all trace of the arm ceased. I was left holding a disembodied arm!

You can imagine my fright. I dropped the arm, tumbled out of bed, and rushed to the balcony calling for help. Melaram was up by then, and he and his boy came rushing to my aid with torches and an old firearm. But there was no one in the room, no remnants of a burnt or dismembered body. And soon it was daylight.

∽

After a few nights in the station hotel, I found a bright, cheerful flat just behind the Odeon cinema. It had electricity too. Although we were subject to long power cuts, I was no longer dependent on the oil lamp, which I still possessed—just in case I couldn't pay the light bills!

But somehow I missed the gentle glow of my oil lamp. I had a feeling that I wrote better by lamplight than by daylight or the harsh light of electricity. The lamp provided the right kind of atmosphere for my writing; it created the mood I wanted, a touch of mystery, a touch of melancholy, of emotions undefined...

The Shadow on the Wall

And so one evening I lit the lamp, sat back on an easy chair, and watched the shadows on the wall.

But there were no shadows apart from mine, no one looking over my shoulder. In the words of the old song, it was just 'my echo, my shadow and me....' And we weren't really company.

I decided to visit a friend at the other end of town. I returned home late. I was too tired to do any work, so I left the lamp burning and went to bed. Outside, on the street, a clock struck twelve.

I was slipping into a dream when I felt that soft hand on my shoulder. Then the other hand touched me. I shivered with fright and apprehension. The hands moved across my chest and arms, there was nothing disembodied about them. I lay perfectly still.

A soft, warm, plump arm brushed against my cheek. I put out my hand to discover, to touch her face. But there was nothing to touch. She was headless!

As I tried to get up, her free arm stretched out, stretched right across the room, and switched off the lamp. I was in bed with a headless woman!

And that's when I woke up. That's when I always wake up. For it's a dream, a nightmare that has pursued me over the years, slowly driving me out of my mind as I try to imagine what the missing head looks like.

THE OVERCOAT

It was clear, frosty weather, and as the moon came up over the Himalayan peaks, I could see that patches of snow still lay on the roads of the hill station. I would have been quite happy in bed, with a book and a hot-water bottle at my side, but I'd promised the Kapadias that I'd go to their party and I felt it would be churlish of me to stay away. I put on two sweaters, an old football scarf, and an overcoat and set off down the moonlit road.

It was a walk of just over a mile to the Kapadias' house and I had covered about half the distance when I saw a girl standing in the middle of the road.

She must have been sixteen or seventeen. She looked rather old-fashioned—long hair, hanging to her waist, and a sequined dress, pink and lavender, that reminded me of the photos in my Grandmother's family album. When I went closer, I noticed that she had lovely eyes and a winning smile.

'Good evening,' I said. 'It's a cold night to be out.'

'Are you going to the party?' she asked.

'That's right. And I can see from your lovely dress that you're going, too. Come along, we're nearly there.'

She fell into step beside me and we soon saw lights from the Kapadias' house shining brightly through the deodars. The girl told me her name was Julie. I hadn't seen her before but then I'd only been in the hill station a few months.

There was quite a crowd at the party but no one seemed to know Julie. Everyone thought she was a friend of mine. I did not deny it. Obviously she was someone who was feeling lonely and wanted to be friendly with people. And she was certainly enjoying herself. I did not see her do much eating or drinking, but she flitted about from one group to another, talking, listening, laughing; and when the music began, she was dancing almost continuously, alone or with partners, it didn't matter which, she was completely wrapped up in the music.

It was almost midnight when I got up to go. I had drunk a fair amount of punch, and I was ready for bed. As I was saying goodnight to my hosts and wishing everyone

The Shadow on the Wall

a merry Christmas, Julie slipped her arm into mine and said she'd be going home, too.

When we were outside, I said, 'Where do you live, Julie?'

'At Wolfsburn,' she said. 'At the top of the hill.'

'There's a cold wind,' I said. 'And although your dress is beautiful, it doesn't look very warm. Here, you'd better wear my overcoat. I've plenty of protection.'

She did not protest and allowed me to slip my overcoat over her shoulders. Then we started out on the walk home. But I did not have to escort her all the way. At about the spot where we had met, she said, 'There's a shortcut from here. I'll just scramble up the hillside.'

'Do you know it well?' I asked. 'It's a very narrow path.'

'Oh, I know every stone on the path. I use it all the time. And besides, it's a really bright night.'

'Well, keep the coat on,' I said. 'I can collect it tomorrow.'

She hesitated for a moment, then smiled and nodded at me. She then disappeared up the hill, and I went home alone.

The next day I walked up to Wolfsburn. I crossed a little brook, from which the house had probably got its name, and entered an open iron gate. But of the house itself little remained. Just a roofless ruin, a pile of stones, a shattered chimney, a few Doric pillars where a veranda had once stood.

Had Julie played a joke on me? Or had I found the wrong house?

I walked around the hill to the mission house where the Taylors lived, and asked old Mrs Taylor if she knew a girl called Julie.

'No, I don't think so,' she said. 'Where does she live?'

'At Wolfsburn, I was told. But the house is just a ruin.'

'Nobody has lived at Wolfsburn for over forty years. The Mackinnons lived there. One of the old families who settled here. But when their girl died...' She stopped and gave me a queer look. 'I think her name was Julie.... Anyway, when she died, they sold the house and went away. No one ever lived in it again, and it fell into decay. But it couldn't be the same Julie you're looking for. She died of consumption—there wasn't much you could do about it in those days. Her grave is in the cemetery, just down the road.'

I thanked Mrs Taylor and walked slowly down the road to the cemetery: not really wanting to know any more, but propelled forward almost against my will.

It was a small cemetery under the deodars. You could see the eternal snows of the Himalaya standing out against the pristine blue of the sky. Here lay the bones of forgotten empire builders—soldiers, merchants, adventurers, their wives and children. It did not take me long to find Julie's grave. It had a simple headstone with her name clearly outlined on it:

Julie Mackinnon
1923–39
With us one moment,
Taken the next
Gone to her Maker,
Gone to her rest.

Although many monsoons had swept across the cemetery wearing down the stones, they had not touched this little tombstone.

I was turning to leave when I caught a glimpse of something familiar behind the headstone. I walked around to where it lay.

Neatly folded on the grass was my overcoat.

THE SKULL

I am not normally bothered by skeletons and old bones—they are, after all, just the chalky remains of the long dead—so that, when my nephew Anil came back from medical college with a well-preserved skull, it was no cause for alarm. He was a second-year student, at times a bit of a prankster.

'I hope you didn't take it without permission,' I said, taking the skull in my hands and admiring its symmetry but without philosophizing upon it like Hamlet.

'Oh, the college is full of them,' said Anil. 'I just borrowed it for the vacation.' He placed it on the mantelpiece, among some of the awards and mementos (cheap brassware mostly) that had accumulated over the years, and I must say it livened up the shelf a little.

Anil had placed the skull at one end of the mantelpiece, and there it stood until we'd had our dinner. He settled down with a book, while I poured myself a small glass of cognac before settling into an easy chair with a notebook on my knee. It was midsummer, and the window was open, so that we could hear the crickets singing in the oak trees. My cottage was on the outskirts of Mussoorie, surrounded by Himalayan oak and maple.

I had been making some notes for an article on wild flowers. When I had finished my notes and cognac, I looked up and noticed that the skull now stood in the centre of the mantelpiece.

'Did you move the skull?' I asked.

'No,' said Anil, looking up. 'I placed it at the end of the shelf.'

'Well, it's now in the middle. How did it get there?'

'You must have moved it yourself, without noticing. That was a stiff cognac you drank, uncle.'

I let it pass, it did not seem important.

∽

People often dropped in to see me. Schoolteachers, visitors to the hill station, students, other writers, neighbours. During that week I had a number of visitors, and of course everyone noticed the skull on the mantelpiece. Some were intrigued, and wanted to know whose skull it was. One or two lady teachers were frightened by it. A fellow writer thought it was in bad taste, displaying human remains in my sitting room. One visitor offered to buy it.

I would gladly have sold the wretched thing, but it belonged to Anil and he intended taking it back to Meerut. But when the time came to leave he forgot about the skull, his mind no doubt taken up with other matters—such as the daily phone calls he received from a girl student in Delhi. After seeing him off at the bus stop, I came home to find that the skull was still occupying pride of place on the mantelpiece.

I ignored it for a few days, and the skull didn't seem to mind that. It was receiving plenty of attention from visitors during the day.

But it was beginning to get on my nerves. Every evening, when I sat down to enjoy a whisky or a cognac, I would feel its empty eye sockets staring at me. And on one occasion, when I tried to change its position, my hand got caught in its jawbone and it was with some difficulty that I withdrew it.

Getting fed up of its presence, I decided to lock the thing away where it wouldn't be seen. There was a wall cupboard in the room, where I kept my manuscripts, notebooks, and writing materials, and there was plenty of room there for the skull. So I shifted it to the cupboard, and made sure the doors were locked.

That evening I enjoyed my drink without being watched by that remnant of a human head. The crickets were singing, a nightjar was calling, and a zephyr of a wind moved softly through the trees. I finished my article and went to bed in a happy frame of mind.

In the middle of the night I woke to a loud rattling sound. At first I thought it was a loose door latch or a wobbly drainpipe; then realized the noise was coming from the wall cupboard. A rat, perhaps? But no. As soon as I opened the cupboard door, out popped the skull, landing near my feet and bouncing away right across the drawing room.

For the sake of peace and quiet, I returned it to the mantelpiece. If a skull could smile, it would probably have done so. I went back to my bed and slept like a baby. It takes more than a dancing skull to keep me from enjoying a good night's sleep.

But next morning I got to work making up a parcel. Normally, I hate making parcels, they usually fall apart. But for once I took pleasure in making a parcel. I wrapped the skull in a plastic bag, then placed it in a strong cardboard box, wrapped this in brown parcel paper, used a liberal amount of Sellotape, and addressed the package to Dr Anil at his medical college. Then I walked into town and handed it over to the registration clerk at the post office.

Rubbing my hands with satisfaction, I treated myself to fish and chips and an ice cream before setting out on the walk down the hill to my cottage.

How did the skull get out of that parcel? I shall never know. Perhaps a nosy postal clerk had opened it to check the contents. I hope he got the fright of his life.

Anyway, I was about halfway down the steep path that leads to one of our famous schools when I heard something rattling down the slope behind me. At first I thought it was an empty tin, but then I recognized my boon companion, that wretched skull, embellished with bits of wrapping paper and Sellotape, bouncing down the hill towards me. I broke into a run, making a dash for the cottage door. But it was there before me, grinning up at me from a pot full of flowering petunias.

So back it went to its favourite place on the mantelpiece. And there it remained for several weeks.

The school's playing field was situated just above the path to the cottage, and during the football season I could hear the boys kicking a football around.

One day a football escaped from the field and came bouncing down the hillside, landing on a flower bed. The match was over and no one bothered to come down to retrieve the ball. But it gave me an idea. I removed the bladder, stuffed the skull into the leather interior, and tied it up firmly. Then I had the football delivered to the school's sports master, with my compliments.

Nothing happened for a couple of days. There was no shortage of footballs. Then in the middle of the game against St George's College, a ball went out of the grounds and a spare one was required.

The replacement did not bounce quite as well as the previous one, and it was inclined to spin around a lot and take off in directions opposite to those intended. Also, it squeaked whenever it received a kick, and sometimes those squeaks sounded a bit like screams of protest. The goalkeepers at either end found the ball difficult to hold, it did its best to elude their grasp. And more goals were scored by accident rather than design. Finally this eccentric ball was kicked out of play and was replaced by another.

What happens to old footballs? I expect they finally fall apart and end up in a dustbin.

The Skull

In this case, the football found a new owner, for the sports master was a kind man who gave away old bats, balls and other worn-out stuff to the poor children of the locality. A boy from a village near Rajpur was the recipient of the battered football, and he and his friends carried it away with a cheer, kicking it all the way down the steep path, making so much noise that they did not hear the groans of protest that issued from the battered old football.

Well, weeks passed, months passed, without the skull making a reappearance. But then something strange began to happen. I found myself missing that troublesome skull!

It had, after all, been company of a sort for a lonely writer living on his own on the edge of the forest. And when you have lived with someone for a long time, then, no matter how much you may quarrel or get on each other's nerves, a bond is formed, and the strength of that bond can only be known when it is broken.

The skull had been sharing my life for over a year, and now that it was gone, seemingly forever, my life seemed rather empty.

So I began searching for the skull. I enquired amongst the children down in Rajpur; but they had long since lost the football. I made a round of all the junk shops in Dehradun, without any luck. There were lots of old footballs lying around, but not the one I wanted. And no, they didn't buy or sell human skulls.

Young Anil, the doctor, paid me a brief visit and found me looking depressed.

'What's the trouble?' he asked. 'You look as though you've just lost a friend.'

'I have, indeed,' I said. 'I miss that skull you gave me. It was company of a sort.'

'Well, I'll get you another. No shortage of skulls in my college.'

'No, I don't want another. I want the same skull. It had a personality of its own.'

Anil looked at me as though he thought I was going off my rocker. And perhaps I was.

And then one day, as I was walking down a busy street in neighbouring Saharanpur, I noticed a fortune teller plying his trade on the pavement. I don't believe in fortune telling, but everyone has to make a living, and telling fortunes seems to me a harmless way of doing it. And then I noticed that he had a skull beside him, and that he would consult it before handing his customer a slip of paper with words of advice or encouragement written on it. It looked a bit like my skull, but I couldn't be sure. All the kicking and manhandling it had received had possibly altered its appearance.

The Skull

But anyway, I gave the fortune teller some money and asked him for a prediction. He chanted something, then extracted a slip of paper from beneath the skull and handed it to me with a flourish.

I read the words printed neatly on the paper.

'Ullu ka patha' went the message, followed by 'Gadhe ka baccha!'

It was definitely my skull! Only an old friend could abuse me like that.

So I pleaded and haggled with the fortune teller, paid him a hundred rupees for the skull, and carried it home in triumph.

And there it is today, decorating my mantelpiece, a little the worse for wear, and with a silly grin on its skeletal face. To improve its looks I have placed an old cricket cap on its head.

Sometimes we don't value our friends until we lose them.

FAIRY GLEN PALACE

The old bridle path from Rajpur to Mussoorie passed through Fosterganj at a height of about five thousand feet. In the old days, before the motor road was built, this was the only road to the hill station. You could ride up on a pony, or walk, or be carried in a basket (if you were a child) or in a doolie (if you were a lady or an invalid). The doolie was a cross between a hammock, a stretcher and a sedan chair, if you can imagine such a contraption. It was borne aloft by two perspiring partners. Sometimes they sat down to rest, and dropped you unceremoniously. I have a picture of my grandmother being borne uphill in a doolie, and she looks petrified. There was an incident in which a doolie, its occupant and two bearers, all went over a cliff just before Fosterganj, and perished in the fall.

Sometimes you can see the ghost of this poor lady being borne uphill by two phantom bearers.

Fosterganj has its ghosts, of course. And they are something of a distraction.

Writing is my vocation, and I have always tried to follow the apostolic maxim: 'Study to be quiet and to mind your own business.' But in small-town India one is constantly drawn into other people's business, just as they are drawn towards yours. In Fosterganj it was quiet enough, there were few people; there was no excuse for shirking work. But tales of haunted houses and fairy-infested forests have always intrigued me, and when I heard that the ruined palace halfway down to Rajpur was a place to be avoided after dark, it was natural for me to start taking my evening walks in its direction.

Fairy Glen was its name. It had been built on the lines of a Swiss or French chalet, with numerous turrets decorating its many wings—a huge, rambling building, two-storeyed, with numerous balconies and cornices and windows; a hodge-podge of architectural styles, a wedding cake of a palace, built to satisfy the whims and fancies of its late owner, the Raja of Ranipur, a small state near the Nepal border. Maintaining this ornate edifice must have been something of a nightmare; and the present heirs had quite given up on it, for bits of the roof were missing, some windows were without panes, doors had developed cracks, and what had once been a garden was now a small jungle. Apparently there was no one living there any more; no sign of a caretaker. I had walked past the wrought-iron gate several times without seeing any signs of life, apart from a large grey cat sunning itself outside a broken window.

Then one evening, walking up from Rajpur, I was caught in a storm.

A wind had sprung up, bringing with it dark, overburdened clouds. Heavy drops of rain were followed by hailstones bouncing off the stony path. Gusts of wind rushed through the oaks, and leaves and small branches were soon swirling through the air. I was still a couple of miles from the Fosterganj bazaar, and I did not fancy sheltering under a tree, as flashes of lightning were beginning to light up the darkening sky. Then I found myself outside the gate of the abandoned palace.

Outside the gate stood an old sentry box. No one had stood sentry in it for years. It was a good place in which to shelter. But I hesitated because a large bird was perched on the gate, seemingly oblivious to the rain that was still falling.

It looked like a crow or a raven, but it was much bigger than either—in fact, twice the size of a crow, but having all the features of one—and when a flash of lightning lit up the gate, it gave a squawk, opened its enormous wings and took off, flying in the direction of the oak forest. I hadn't seen such a bird before; there was something dark and malevolent and almost supernatural about it. But it had gone, and I darted into the sentry box without further delay.

I had been standing there some ten minutes, wondering when the rain was going to stop, when I heard someone running down the road. As he approached, I could see that he was just a boy, probably eleven or twelve; but in the dark I could not make out his features. He came up to the gate, lifted the latch, and was about to go in when he saw me in the sentry box.

'Kaun? Who are you?' he asked, first in Hindi then in English. He did not appear to be in any way anxious or alarmed.

'Just sheltering from the rain,' I said. 'I live in the bazaar.' He took a small torch from his pocket and shone it in my face.

'Yes, I have seen you there. A tourist.'

'A writer. I stay in places, I don't just pass through.'

'Do you want to come in?'

I hesitated. It was still raining and the roof of the sentry box was leaking badly.

'Do you live here?' I asked.

'Yes, I am the raja's nephew. I live here with my mother. Come in.' He took me by the hand and led me through the gate. His hand was quite rough and heavy for an eleven- or twelve-year-old. Instead of walking with me to the front steps and entrance of the old palace, he led me around to the rear of the building, where a faint light glowed in a mullioned window, and in its light I saw that he had a very fresh and pleasant face—a face as yet untouched by the trials of life.

Instead of knocking on the door, he tapped on the window.

'Only strangers knock on the door,' he said. 'When I tap on the window, my mother knows it's me.'

'That's clever of you,' I said.

He tapped again, and the door was opened by an unusually tall woman wearing a kind of loose, flowing gown that looked strange in that place, and on her. The light was behind her, and I couldn't see her face until we had entered the room. When she turned to me, I saw that she had a long reddish scar running down one side of her face. Even so, there was a certain, hard beauty in her appearance.

'Make some tea—Mother,' said the boy rather brusquely.

'And something to eat. I'm hungry. Sir, will you have something?' He looked enquiringly at me. The light from a kerosene lamp fell full on his face. He was wide-eyed, full-lipped, smiling; only his voice seemed rather mature for one so young. And he spoke like someone much older, and with an almost unsettling sophistication.

'Sit down, sir.' He led me to a chair, made me comfortable. 'You are not too wet, I hope?'

'No, I took shelter before the rain came down too heavily. But you are wet, you'd better change.'

'It doesn't bother me.' And after a pause, 'Sorry there is no electricity. Bills haven't been paid for years.'

'Is this your place?'

'No, we are only caretakers. Poor relations, you might say. The palace has been in dispute for many years. The raja and his brothers keep fighting over it, and meanwhile it is slowly falling down. The lawyers are happy. Perhaps I should study and become a lawyer some day.'

'Do you go to school?'

'Sometimes.'

'How old are you?'

'Quite old, I'm not sure. Mother, how old am I?' he asked, as the tall woman returned with cups of tea and a plateful of biscuits.

She hesitated, gave him a puzzled look. 'Don't you

know? It's on your certificate.'

'I've lost the certificate.'

'No, I've kept it safely.' She looked at him intently, placed a hand on his shoulder, then turned to me and said, 'He is twelve,' with a certain finality.

We finished our tea. It was still raining.

'It will rain all night,' said the boy. 'You had better stay here.'

'It will inconvenience you.'

'No, it won't. There are many rooms. If you do not mind the darkness. Come, I will show you everything. And meanwhile my mother will make some dinner. Very simple food, I hope you won't mind.'

The boy took me around the old palace, if you could still call it that. He led the way with a candleholder from which a large candle threw our exaggerated shadows on the walls.

'What's your name?' I asked, as he led me into what must have been a reception room, still crowded with ornate furniture and bric-a-brac.

'Bhim,' he said. 'But everyone calls me Lucky.'

'And are you lucky?'

He shrugged. 'Don't know....' Then he smiled up at me. 'Maybe you'll bring me luck.'

We walked further into the room. Large oil

Fairy Glen Palace

paintings hung from the walls, gathering mould. Some were portraits of royalty, kings and queens of another era, wearing decorative headgear, strange uniforms, the women wrapped in jewellery—more jewels than garments, it seemed—and sometimes accompanied by children who were also weighed down by excessive clothing. A young man sat on a throne, his lips curled in a sardonic smile.

'My grandfather,' said Bhim.

He led me into a large bedroom taken up by a four-poster bed which had probably seen several royal couples copulating upon it. It looked cold and uninviting, but Bhim produced a voluminous razai from a cupboard and assured me that it would be warm and quite luxurious, as it had been his grandfather's.

'And when did your grandfather die?' I asked.

'Oh, fifty-sixty years ago, it must have been.'

'In this bed, I suppose.'

'No, he was shot accidentally while out hunting. They said it was an accident. But he had enemies.'

'Kings have enemies.... And this was the royal bed?'

He gave me a sly smile; not so innocent after all. 'Many women slept in it. He had many queens.'

'And concubines.'

'What are concubines?'

'Unofficial queens.'
'Yes, those too.'
A worldly-wise boy of twelve.

⁌

A BIG BLACK BIRD
I did not feel like sleeping in that room, with its musty old draperies and paint peeling off the walls. A trickle of water from the ceiling fell down the back of my shirt and made me shiver.

'The roof is leaking,' I said. 'Maybe I'd better go home.'

'You can't go now, it's very late. And that leopard has been seen again.'

He fetched a china bowl from the dressing table and placed it on the floor to catch the trickle from the ceiling. In another corner of the room a metal bucket was receiving a steady patter from another leak.

'The palace is leaking everywhere,' said Bhim cheerfully. 'This is the only dry room.'

He took me by the hand and led me back to his own quarters. I was surprised, again, by how heavy and rough his hand was for a boy, and presumed that he did a certain amount of manual work such as chopping wood for a daily fire. In winter the building would be unbearably cold.

His mother gave us a satisfying meal, considering the ingredients at her disposal were somewhat limited. Once again, I tried to get away. But only half-heartedly. The boy intrigued me; so did his mother; so did the rambling old palace; and the rain persisted.

Bhim the Lucky took me to my room; waited with the guttering candle till I had removed my shoes; handed me a pair of very large pyjamas.

'Royal pyjamas,' he said with a smile.

I got into them and floated around.

'Before you go—' I said. 'I might want to visit the bathroom in the night.'

'Of course, sir. It's close by.' He opened a door, and beyond it I saw a dark passage. 'Go a little way, and there's a door on the left. I'm leaving an extra candle and matches on the dressing table.'

He put the lighted candle he was carrying on the table, and left the room without a light. Obviously he knew his way about in the dark. His footsteps receded, and I was left alone with the sound of raindrops pattering on the roof and a loose sheet of corrugated tin roofing flapping away in a wind that had now sprung up.

It was a summer's night, and I had no need of blankets;

so I removed my shoes and jacket and lay down on the capacious bed, wondering if I should blow the candle out or allow it to burn as long as it lasted.

Had I been in my own room, I would have been reading—a Conrad or a Chekhov or some other classic—because at night I turn to the classics—but here there was no light and nothing to read.

I got up and blew the candle out. I might need it later on.

Restless, I prowled around the room in the dark, banging into chairs and footstools. I made my way to the window and drew the curtains aside. Some light filtered into the room because behind the clouds there was a moon, and it had been a full moon the night before.

I lay back on the bed. It wasn't very comfortable. It was a box-bed, of the sort that had only just begun to become popular in households with small bedrooms. This one had been around for some time—no doubt a very early version of its type—and although it was covered with a couple of thick mattresses, the woodwork appeared to have warped because it creaked loudly whenever I shifted my position. The boards no longer fitted properly. Either that, or the box-bed had been overstuffed with all sorts of things.

After some time I settled into one position and dozed

off for a while, only to be awakened by the sound of someone screaming somewhere in the building. My hair stood on end. The screaming continued, and I wondered if I should get up to investigate. Then suddenly it stopped—broke off in the middle as though it had been muffled by a hand or piece of cloth.

There was a tapping at the pane of the big French window in front of the bed. Probably the branch of a tree, swaying in the wind. But then there was a screech, and I sat up in bed. Another screech, and I was out of it.

I went to the window and pressed my face to the glass. The big black bird—the bird I had seen when taking shelter in the sentry box—was sitting, or rather squatting, on the boundary wall, facing me. The moon, now visible through the clouds, fell full upon it. I had never seen a bird like it before. Crow-like, but heavily built, like a turkey, its beak that of a bird of prey, its talons those of a vulture. I stepped back, and closed the heavy curtains, shutting out the light but also shutting out the image of that menacing bird.

Returning to the bed, I just sat there for a while, wondering if I should get up and leave. The rain had lessened. But the luminous dial of my watch showed it was two in the morning. No time for a stroll in the dark—not with a man-eating leopard in the vicinity.

Then I heard the shriek again. It seemed to echo through the building. It may have been the bird, but to me it sounded all too human. There was silence for a long while after that. I lay back on the bed and tried to sleep. But it was even more uncomfortable than before. Perhaps the wood had warped too much during the monsoon, I thought, and the lid of the old box-bed did not fit properly. Maybe I could push it back into its correct position; then perhaps I could get some sleep.

So I got up again, and after fumbling around in the dark for a few minutes, found the matches and lit the candle. Then I removed the sheets from the bed and pulled away the two mattresses. The cover of the box-bed lay exposed. And a hand protruded from beneath the lid.

It was not a living hand. It was a skeletal hand, fleshless, brittle. But there was a ring on one finger, an opal still clinging to the bone of a small index finger. It glowed faintly in the candlelight.

Shaking a little (for I am really something of a coward, though an inquisitive one), I lifted the lid of the box-bed. Laid out on a pretty counterpane was a skeleton. A bundle of bones, but still clothed in expensive-looking garments. One hand gripped the side of the box-bed; the hand that had kept it from shutting properly.

I dropped the lid of the box-bed and ran from the

room—only to blunder into a locked door. Someone, presumably the boy, had locked me into the bedroom.

I banged on the door and shouted, but no one heard me. No one came running. I went to the large French window, but it was firmly fastened, it probably hadn't been opened for many years.

Then I remembered the passageway leading to the bathroom. The boy had pointed it out to me. Possibly there was a way out from there.

There was. It was an old door that opened easily, and I stepped out into the darkness, finding myself entangled in a creeper that grew against the wall. From its cloying fragrance I recognized it as wisteria.

A narrow path led to a wicket-gate at the end of the building. I found my way out of the grounds and back on the familiar public road. The old palace loomed out of the darkness. I turned my back on it and set off for home, my little room above Hassan's bakery.

Nothing happens in Fosterganj, I told myself. But something had happened in that old palace.

EYES OF THE CAT

Her eyes seemed flecked with gold when the sun was on them. And as the sun set over the mountains, drawing a deep red wound across the sky, there was more than gold in Kiran's eyes. There was anger; for she had been cut to the quick by some remarks her teacher had made—the culmination of weeks of insults and taunts.

Kiran was poorer than most of the girls in her class and could not afford the tuitions that had become almost obligatory if one was to pass and be promoted. 'You'll have to spend another year in the ninth,' said Madam. 'And if you don't like that, you can find another school—a school where it won't matter if your blouse is torn and your tunic is old and your shoes are falling apart.' Madam had shown her large teeth in what was supposed to be a good-natured smile, and all the girls had tittered dutifully. Sycophancy had become part of the curriculum in Madam's private academy for girls.

On the way home in the gathering gloom, Kiran's two companions commiserated with her.

'She's a mean old thing,' said Aarti. 'She doesn't care for anyone but herself.'

'Her laugh reminds me of a donkey braying,' said Sunita, who was more forthright.

But Kiran wasn't really listening. Her eyes were fixed on some point in the far distance, where the pines stood in silhouette against a night sky that was growing brighter every moment. The moon was rising, a full moon, a moon that meant something very special to Kiran, that made her blood tingle and her skin prickle and her hair glow and send out sparks. Her steps seemed to grow lighter, her limbs more sinewy as she moved gracefully, softly over the mountain path.

Abruptly she left her companions at a fork in the road.

'I'm taking the shortcut through the forest,' she said.

Her friends were used to her sudden whims. They knew she was not afraid of being alone in the dark. But Kiran's moods made them feel a little nervous, and now, holding hands, they hurried home along the open road.

The shortcut took Kiran through the dark oak forest.

The Shadow on the Wall

The crooked, tormented branches of the oaks threw twisted shadows across the path. A jackal howled at the moon; a nightjar called from urgency, and her breath came in short, sharp gasps. Bright moonlight bathed the hillside when she reached her home on the outskirts of the village.

Refusing her dinner, she went straight to her small room and flung the window open. Moonbeams crept over the windowsill and over her arms which were already covered with golden hair. Her strong nails had shredded the rotten wood of the windowsill.

Tail swishing and ears pricked, the tawny leopard came swiftly out of the window, crossed the open field behind the house, and melted into the shadows.

A little later it padded silently through the forest.

Although the moon shone brightly on the tin-roofed town, the leopard knew where the shadows were deepest and merged beautifully with them. An occasional intake of breath, which resulted in a short rasping cough, was the only sound it made.

Madam was returning from dinner at a ladies' club, called the Kitten Club as a sort of foil to the husbands' club affiliations. There were still a few people in the street, and while no one could help noticing Madam, who had the contours of a steamroller, none saw or heard the predator who had slipped down a side alley and reached the steps of the teacher's house. It sat there silently, waiting with all the patience of an obedient schoolgirl.

When Madam saw the leopard on her steps, she dropped her handbag and opened her mouth to scream; but her voice would not materialize. Nor would her tongue ever be used again, either to savour chicken biryani or to pour scorn upon her pupils, for the leopard had sprung at her throat, broken her neck, and dragged her into the bushes.

In the morning, when Aarti and Sunita set out for school, they stopped as usual at Kiran's cottage and called out to her.

Kiran was sitting in the sun, combing her long black hair.

'Aren't you coming to school today, Kiran?' asked the girls.

'No, I won't bother to go today,' said Kiran. She felt lazy, but pleased with herself, like a contented cat.

'Madam won't be pleased,' said Aarti. 'Shall we tell her you're sick?'

'It won't be necessary,' said Kiran, and gave them one of her mysterious smiles. 'I'm sure it's going to be a holiday.'

SUSANNA'S SEVEN HUSBANDS

Locally, the tomb was known as 'the grave of the seven-times married one'.

You'd be forgiven for thinking it was Bluebeard's grave; he was reputed to have killed several wives in turn because they showed undue curiosity about a locked room. But this was the tomb of Susanna Anna-Maria Yeates, and the inscription (most of it in Latin) stated that she was mourned by all who had benefited from her generosity, her beneficiaries having included various schools, orphanages, and the church across the road. There was no sign of any other graves in the vicinity, and presumably her husbands had been interred in the old Rajpur graveyard, below the Delhi Ridge.

I was still in my teens when I first saw the ruins of

what had once been a spacious and handsome mansion. Desolate and silent, its well-laid paths were overgrown with weeds, its flower beds had disappeared under a growth of thorny jungle. The two-storeyed house had looked across the Grand Trunk Road. Now abandoned, feared, and shunned, it stood encircled in mystery, reputedly the home of evil spirits.

Outside the gate, along the Grand Trunk Road, thousands of vehicles sped by—cars, trucks, buses, tractors, bullock carts—but few noticed the old mansion or its mausoleum, set back as they were from the main road, hidden by mango, neem, and peepul trees. One old and massive peepul tree grew out of the ruins of the house, strangling it as much as its owner was said to have strangled one of her dispensable paramours.

As a much-married person with a quaint habit of disposing of her husbands, whenever she tired of them, Susanna's malignant spirit was said to haunt the deserted garden. I had examined the tomb, I had gazed upon the ruins, I had scrambled through shrubbery and overgrown rose bushes, but I had not encountered the spirit of this mysterious woman. Perhaps, at the time, I was too pure and innocent to be targeted by malignant spirits. For, malignant she must have been, if the stories about her were true.

The Shadow on the Wall

The vaults of the ruined mansion were rumoured to contain a buried treasure—the amassed wealth of the lady Susanna. But no one dared go down there, for the vaults were said to be occupied by a family of cobras, traditional guardians of buried treasure. Had she really been a woman of great wealth, and could treasure still be buried there? I put these questions to Naushad, the furniture maker, who had lived in the vicinity all his life, and whose father had made the furniture and fittings for this and other great houses in Old Delhi.

'Lady Susanna, as she was known, was much sought after for her wealth,' recalled Naushad. 'She was no miser, either. She spent freely, reigning in state in her palatial home, with many horses and carriages at her disposal. Every evening she rode through the Roshanara Gardens, the cynosure of all eyes, for she was beautiful as well as wealthy. Yes, all men sought her favours, and she could choose from the best of them. Many were fortune hunters. She did not discourage them. Some found favour for a time, but she soon tired of them. None of her husbands enjoyed her wealth for very long!

'Today, no one enters those ruins, where once there was mirth and laughter. She was a zamindari lady, the owner of much land, and she administered her estate with a strong hand. She was kind if rents were paid when they fell due, but terrible if someone failed to pay.

'Well, over fifty years have gone by since she was laid to rest, but still men speak of her with awe. Her spirit is restless, and it is said that she often visits the scenes of her former splendour. She has been seen walking through this gate, or riding in the gardens, or driving in her phaeton down the Rajpur Road.'

'And, what happened to all those husbands?' I asked.

'Most of them died mysterious deaths. Even the doctors were baffled. Tomkins Sahib drank too much. The lady soon tired of him. A drunken husband is a burdensome creature, she was heard to say. He would eventually have drunk himself to death, but she was an impatient woman and was anxious to replace him. You see those datura bushes growing wild in the grounds? They have always done well here.'

'Belladonna?' I suggested.

'That's right, huzoor. Introduced in the whisky-soda, they put him to sleep forever.'

'She was quite humane in her way.'

'Oh, very humane, sir. She hated to see anyone suffer. One sahib, I don't know his name, drowned in the tank behind the house, where the water lilies grew. But she made sure he was half-dead before he fell in. She had large, powerful hands, they said.'

'Why did she bother to marry them? Couldn't she just have had men friends?'

'Not in those days, dear sir. Respectable society would not have tolerated it. Neither in India nor in the West would it have been permitted.'

'She was born out of her time,' I remarked.

'True, sir. And remember, most of them were fortune hunters. So, we need not waste too much pity on them.'

'She did not waste any.'

'She was without pity. Especially when she found out what they were really after. The snakes had a better chance of survival.'

'How did the other husbands take their leave of this world?'

'Well, the Colonel sahib shot himself while cleaning his rifle. Purely an accident, huzoor. Although some say she had loaded his gun without his knowledge. Such was her reputation by now that she was suspected even when innocent. But she bought her way out of trouble. It was easy enough, if you were wealthy.'

'And, the fourth husband?'

'Oh, he died a natural death. There was a cholera epidemic that year, and he was carried off by the haija. Although, again, there were some who said that a good dose of arsenic produced the same symptoms! Anyway, it was cholera on the death certificate. And, the doctor who signed it was the next to marry her.'

'Being a doctor, he was probably quite careful about what he ate and drank.

'He lasted about a year.'

'What happened?'

'He was bitten by a cobra.'

'Well, that was just bad luck, wasn't it? You could hardly blame it on Susanna.'

'No, huzoor, but the cobra was in his bedroom. It was coiled around the bedpost. And, when he undressed for the night, it struck! He was dead when Susanna came into the room an hour later. She had a way with snakes. She did not harm them and they never attacked her.'

'And, there were no antidotes in those days. Exit the doctor. Who was the sixth husband?'

'A handsome man. An indigo planter. He had gone bankrupt when the indigo trade came to an end. He was hoping to recover his fortune with the good lady's help. But our Susanna memsahib, she did not believe in sharing her fortune with anyone.'

'How did she remove the indigo planter?'

'It was said that she lavished strong drink upon him, and when he lay helpless, she assisted him on the road we all have to take by pouring molten lead in his ears.'

'A painless death, I'm told.'

'But a terrible price to pay, huzoor, simply because one is no longer needed...'

We walked along the dusty highway, enjoying the evening breeze, and some time later we entered the Roshanara Gardens, in those days Delhi's most popular and fashionable meeting place.

'You have told me how six of her husbands died, Naushad. I thought there were seven?'

'Ah, the seventh was a gallant young magistrate, who perished right here, huzoor. They were driving through the park after dark when the lady's carriage was attacked by brigands. In defending her, the young man received a fatal sword wound.'

'Not the lady's fault, Naushad.'

'No, huzoor. But he was a magistrate, remember, and the assailants, one of whose relatives had been convicted by him, were out for revenge. Oddly enough, though, two of the men were given employment by the lady Susanna at a later date. You may draw your own conclusions.'

'And, were there others?'

'Not husbands. But an adventurer, a soldier of fortune came along. He found her treasure, they say. And he lies buried with it, in the cellars of the ruined house. His bones lie scattered there, among gold and silver and other precious jewels. The cobras guard them still! But how he perished was a mystery, and remains so till this day.'

'And Susanna? What happened to her?'

'She lived to a ripe old age. If she paid for her crimes, it wasn't in this life! She had no children, but she started an orphanage and gave generously to the poor and to various schools and institutions, including a home for widows. She died peacefully in her sleep.'

'A merry widow,' I remarked. 'The Black Widow spider!'

Don't go looking for Susanna's tomb. It vanished some years ago, along with the ruins of her mansion. A smart new housing estate came up on the site, but not before several workmen and a contractor succumbed to snake bites! Occasionally, residents complain of a malignant ghost in their midst, who is given to flagging down cars, especially those driven by single men. There have also been one or two mysterious disappearances.

And, after dusk, an old-fashioned horse and carriage can sometimes be seen driving through the Roshanara Gardens. If you chance upon it, ignore it, my friend. Don't stop to answer any questions from the beautiful fair lady who smiles at you from behind lace curtains. She's still looking for her final victim.

WHISPERING IN THE DARK

A wild night. Wind moaning, trees lashing themselves in a frenzy, rain beating down on the road, thunder over the mountains. Loneliness stretched ahead of me, a loneliness of the heart as well as a physical loneliness. The world was blotted out by a mist that had come up from the valley, a thick, white, clammy shroud.

I groped through the forest, groped in my mind for the memory of a mountain path, some remembered rock or ancient deodar. Then a streak of blue lightning gave me a glimpse of a barren hillside and a house cradled in mist.

It was an old-world house, built of limestone rock on the outskirts of a crumbling hill station. There was no light in its windows; probably the electricity had been disconnected long ago. But if I could get in, it would do for the night.

I had no torch, but at times the moon shone through the wild clouds, and trees loomed out of the mist like primeval giants. I reached the front door and found it locked from within. I walked round to the side and broke a windowpane, put my hand through shattered glass and found the bolt.

The window, warped by over a hundred monsoons, resisted at first. Then it yielded, and I climbed into the mustiness of a long-closed room, and the wind came in with me, scattering papers across the floor and knocking some unidentifiable object off a table. I closed the window, bolted it again, but the mist crawled through the broken glass, and the wind rattled in it like a pair of castanets.

There were matches in my pocket. I struck three before a light flared up.

I was in a large room, crowded with furniture. Pictures on the walls. Vases on the mantelpiece. A candlestand. And, strangely enough, no cobwebs. For all its external look of neglect and dilapidation, the house had been cared for by someone. But before I could notice anything else, the match burnt out.

As I stepped further into the room, the old deodar flooring creaked beneath my weight. By the light of another match I reached the mantelpiece and lit the candle, noticing at the same time that the candlestick was a genuine antique with cutglass hangings. A deserted cottage with good furniture and glass. I wondered why no one had ever broken in. And then realized that I had just done so.

I held the candlestick high and glanced round the room. The walls were hung with several watercolours and portraits in oils. There was no dust anywhere. But no one answered my call, no one responded to my hesitant knocking. It was as though the occupants of the house were in hiding, watching me obliquely from dark corners and chimneys.

I entered a bedroom and found myself facing a full-length mirror. My reflection stared back at me as though I were a stranger, as though my reflection belonged to the house, while I was only an outsider.

As I turned from the mirror, I thought I saw someone, something, some reflection other than mine, move behind me in the mirror. I caught a glimpse of whiteness, a pale oval face, burning eyes, long tresses, golden in the candlelight. But when I looked in the mirror again there was nothing to be seen but my own pallid face.

A pool of water was forming at my feet. I set the candle down on a small table, found the edge of the bed—a large old four-poster—sat down, and removed my soggy shoes and socks. Then I took off my clothes and hung them over the back of a chair.

I stood naked in the darkness, shivering a little. There was no one to see me—and yet I felt oddly exposed, almost as though I had stripped in a room full of curious people.

I got under the bedclothes—they smelt slightly of eucalyptus and lavender—but found there was no pillow. That was odd. A perfectly made bed, but no pillow! I was too tired to hunt for one. So, I blew out the candle and the darkness closed in around me, and the whispering began…

The whispering began as soon as I closed my eyes. I couldn't tell where it came from. It was all around me, mingling with the sound of the wind coughing in the chimney, the stretching of old furniture, the weeping of trees outside in the rain.

Sometimes I could hear what was being said. The words came from a distance: a distance not so much of space as of time…

'Mine, mine, he is all mine…'

'He is ours, dear, ours.'

Whispers, echoes, words hovering around me with bats' wings, saying the most inconsequential things with a logical urgency. 'You're late for supper…'

'He lost his way in the mist.'

'Do you think he has any money?'

'To kill a turtle you must first tie its legs to two posts.'

'We could tie him to the bed and pour boiling water down his throat.'

'No, it's simpler this way.'

I sat up. Most of the whispering had been distant, impersonal, but this last remark had sounded horribly near.

I relit the candle and the voices stopped. I got up and prowled around the room, vainly looking for some explanation for the voices. Once again I found myself facing the mirror, staring at my own reflection and the reflection of that other person, the girl with the golden hair and shining eyes. And this time she held a pillow in her hands. She was standing behind me.

I remembered then the stories I had heard as a boy, of two spinster sisters—one beautiful, one plain—who lured rich, elderly gentlemen into their boarding house and suffocated them in the night. The deaths had appeared quite natural, and they had got away with it for years. It was only the surviving sister's deathbed confession that had revealed the truth—and even then no one had believed her.

But that had been many, many years ago, and the house had long since fallen down...

When I turned from the mirror, there was no one behind me. I looked again, and the reflection had gone.

I crawled back into the bed and put the candle out. And I slept and dreamt (or was I awake and did it really happen?) that the woman I had seen in the mirror stood beside the bed, leant over me, looked at me with eyes flecked by orange flames. I saw people moving in those eyes. I saw myself. And then her lips touched mine, lips so cold, so dry, that a shudder ran through my body.

And then, while her face became faceless and only the eyes remained, something else continued to press down upon me, something soft, heavy, and shapeless, enclosing me in a suffocating embrace. I could not turn my head or open my mouth. I could not breathe.

I raised my hands and clutched feebly at the thing on top of me. And to my surprise it came away. It was only a pillow that had somehow fallen over my face, half suffocating me while I dreamt of a phantom kiss.

I flung the pillow aside. I flung the bedclothes from me. I had had enough of whispering, of ownerless reflections, of pillows that fell on me in the dark. I would brave the storm outside rather than continue to seek rest in this tortured house.

I dressed quickly. The candle had almost guttered out. The house and everything in it belonged to the darkness of another time; I belonged to the light of day.

I was ready to leave. I avoided the tall mirror with its

grotesque rococo design. Holding the candlestick before me, I moved cautiously into the front room. The pictures on the walls sprang to life.

One, in particular, held my attention, and I moved closer to examine it more carefully by the light of the dwindling candle. Was it just my imagination, or was the girl in the portrait the woman of my dream, the beautiful pale reflection in the mirror? Had I gone back in time, or had time caught up with me? Is it time that's passing by, or is it you and I?

I turned to leave, and the candle gave one final sputter and went out, plunging the room in darkness. I stood still for a moment, trying to collect my thoughts, to still the panic that came rushing upon me. Just then there was a knocking on the door.

'Who's there?' I called.

Silence. And then, again, the knocking, and this time a voice, low and insistent: 'Please let me in, please let me in…'

I stepped forward, unbolted the door, and flung it open.

She stood outside in the rain. Not the pale, beautiful one, but a wizened old hag with bloodless lips and flaring nostrils and—but where were the eyes? No eyes, no eyes!

She swept past me on the wind, and at the same time I took advantage of the open doorway to run outside, to run gratefully into the pouring rain, to be lost for hours among the dripping trees, to be glad for all the leeches clinging to my flesh.

And when, with the dawn, I found my way at last, I rejoiced in birdsong and the sunlight piercing and scattering the clouds.

And today if you were to ask me if the old house is still there or not, I would not be able to tell you, for the simple reason that I haven't the slightest desire to go looking for it.

THE CHAKRATA CAT

The Chakrata is a small hill station roughly midway between Shimla and Mussoorie. During my youth, before the road became motorable, I would trek from one hill station to the other, sometimes alone, sometimes in company. It would take me about five days to cover the distance. I was a leisurely walker. You couldn't enjoy a hike if you felt you had to catch a train at the end of it.

At Chakrata, there was an old forest rest house where I would sometimes spend the night. Don't go looking for it now. It has fallen into disuse and been replaced by a new building closer to the town.

Towards sunset, late that summer, I trudged upto the rest house and called out for the chowkidar. I forget his name. He was a grizzled old man, uncommunicative. If you told him you had just been chased by a bear, he would simply nod and say, 'You'd better rest, then. You must be tried,' Nothing about the bear!

Anyway, he opened up one of the bedrooms for me, prepared a modest meal (which I enjoyed, having eaten little all day), and offered to make a fire in the old fireplace.

Chakrata can be cold, even in September, and I offered to pay for the firewood if he would fetch some. He switched on the bedroom and veranda lights and then walked to the rear of the building to fetch some wood.

That was when I saw the cat.

It was a large black cat, and it was sitting before the fireplace, almost as though expecting a fire to be lit. I hadn't noticed it entering the room, and it did not pay much attention to me, just kept staring into the fireplace. Then, when it heard the chowkidar returning, it got up and left the room.

'You have a cat?' I asked, trying to make conversation while he lit the fire.

He shook his head. 'Cats come for rats,' he said, which left me no wiser. And he took off, promising to bring me a cup of tea early next morning. There was a small bookshelf in a corner of room, and I found an old favourite, *A Warning to the Curious* by M. R. James. His haunting stories of ghosts in old colleges kept me awake for a couple of hours; then I put out the light and got into bed.

I had quite forgotten about the cat.

Now I heard a soft purring as the cat jumped on to the bed and curled up near my feet. I am not particularly fond of cats, and my first impulse was to kick it off the bed. Then I thought, 'Well, it's probably used to sleeping in this room, especially with the fire lit. I'll let it be, as long as it doesn't start chasing rats in the middle of the night!' And all it did was come a little closer to me, advancing from my feet to my knees, and purring loudly, as though quite satisfied with the situation.

I fell asleep and slept soundly. In fact, I must have slept for a couple of hours before I woke to a feeling of wetness under my armpit. My vest was wet, and something was sucking away at my flesh.

It was with a feeling of horror that I realized that the cat had crawled into bed with me, that it was now stretched out beside me, and that it was licking away at my armpit with a certain amount of relish. For the purring was louder than ever.

I sat up in bed, flung the cat from me, and made a dash for the light switch. As the light came on, I saw the cat standing at the foot of the bed, tail erect and hair on end. It was very angry. And then, for the space of five seconds at the most, its appearance changed and its head was that of a human—a woman, black-browed with flaring nostrils and large crooked ears, her lips full and drenched with blood—my blood!

The moment passed and it was a cat's head once again. She let out a howl, sprang from the bed, and disappeared through the bathroom door.

My shirt and vest were soaked with blood. For over an hour the cat had been licking and sucking at my fragile skin, wearing it away until the blood oozed out. Cat or vampire or witches revenant? Or a combination of all three.

I went to the bathroom. The cat had taken off through an open window. I closed the window, bathed my wound, examined myself in the mirror.

I had not been bitten. These were no teeth marks, no scratches. The tongue, and constant licking, had done the damage.

I found some cotton wool in my haversack, and used it to stop the trickle of blood from my armpit. Then I changed my vest and shirt, and sat down on an easy chair to wait for the dawn. It was three in the morning. I felt weak and fell asleep in my chair, to be awakened by the chowkidar knocking on my door with a cup of tea.

Chakrata is a lovely place, prettier than most hill

stations, but I had no desire to linger there. There was a bus to Dehradun at eight o'clock. I decided to cut short my trek and take the bus.

'Where's that cat of yours?' I asked the chowkidar before I left. He knew nothing about a cat. Did not care for cats. They were unlucky, the companions of evil spirits, creatures of the world of dead.

I did not stop to argue, but thanked him for his hospitality and took my leave.

The wound, if you can call it that, took some time to heal. The skin beneath my armpit was all crinkly for a few weeks, but the body heals itself, if given a chance to do so.

But what remains on my skin is a bright red mark, the size and shape of a cat's tongue. It's been there all these years and won't go away. I'll show it to you, the next time you come to see me.

A FACE IN THE DARK

Mr Oliver, an Anglo-Indian teacher, was returning to his school late one night, on the outskirts of the hill station of Shimla. From before Kipling's time, the school had been run on English public school lines and the boys, most of them from wealthy Indian families, wore blazers, caps, and ties. *Life* magazine, in a feature on India, had once called this school the 'Eton of the East'. Mr Oliver had been teaching in the school for several years.

The Shimla bazaar, with its cinemas and restaurants, was about three miles from the school; and Mr Oliver, a bachelor, usually strolled into the town in the evening, returning after dark, when he would take a shortcut through the pine forest.

When there was a strong wind, the pine trees made

The Shadow on the Wall

sad, eerie sounds that kept most people to the main road. But Mr Oliver was not a nervous or imaginative man. He carried a torch and its gleam—the batteries were running down—moved fitfully down the narrow forest path. When its flickering light fell on the figure of a boy, who was sitting alone on a rock, Mr Oliver stopped. Boys were not supposed to be out after dark.

'What are you doing out here, boy?' asked Mr Oliver sharply, moving closer so that he could recognize the miscreant. But even as he approached the boy, Mr Oliver sensed that something was wrong. The boy appeared to be crying. His head hung down, he held his face in his hands, and his body shook convulsively. It was a strange, soundless weeping, and Mr Oliver felt distinctly uneasy.

'Well, what's the matter?' he asked, his anger giving way to concern. 'What are you crying for?' The boy would not answer or look up. His body continued to be racked with silent sobbing. 'Come on, boy, you shouldn't be out here at this hour. Tell me the trouble. Look up!' The boy looked up. He took his hands from his face and looked up at his teacher. The light from Mr Oliver's torch fell on the boy's face—if you could call it a face.

It had no eyes, ears, nose, or mouth. It was just a round smooth head—with a school cap on top of it! And

A Face in the Dark

that's where the story should end. But for Mr Oliver it did not end there.

The torch fell from his trembling hand. He turned and scrambled down the path, running blindly through the trees and calling for help. He was still running towards the school buildings when he saw a lantern swinging in the middle of the path. Mr Oliver stumbled up to the watchman, gasping for breath. 'What is it, sahib?' asked the watchman. 'Has there been an accident? Why are you running?'

'I saw something—something horrible—a boy weeping in the forest—and he had no face!'

'No face, sahib?'

'No eyes, nose, mouth—nothing.'

'Do you mean it was like this, sahib?' asked the watchman and raised the lamp to his own face. The watchman had no eyes, no ears, no features at all—not even an eyebrow! And that's when the wind blew the lamp out.

GHOST TROUBLE

I

It was Grandfather who finally decided that we would have to move to another house.

And it was all because of a pret, a mischievous north Indian ghost, who had been making life difficult for everyone.

Prets usually live in peepul trees, and that's where our little ghost first had his home—in the branches of a massive old peepul tree which had grown through the compound wall and spread into our garden. Part of the tree was on our side of the wall, part on the other side, shading the main road. It gave the ghost a good view of the whole area.

Ghost Trouble

For many years the pret had lived there quite happily, without bothering anyone in our house. He did not bother me, either, and I spent a lot of time in the peepul tree. Sometimes I went there to escape the adults at home, sometimes to watch the road and the people who passed by. The peepul tree was cool on a hot day, and the heart-shaped leaves were always waving in the breeze. This constant movement of the leaves also helped to disguise the movements of the pret, so that I never really knew exactly where he was sitting. But he paid no attention to me. The traffic on the road kept him fully occupied.

Sometimes, when a tonga was passing, he would jump down and frighten the pony, and as a result the little pony cart would go rushing off in the wrong direction.

Sometimes, he would get into the engine of a car or a bus, which would have a breakdown soon afterwards.

And he liked to knock the sun helmets off the heads of sahibs or officials, who would wonder how a strong breeze had sprung up so suddenly, only to die down just as quickly. Although this special kind of ghost could make himself felt, and sometimes heard, he was invisible to the human eye.

I was not invisible to the human eye, and often got the blame for some of the pret's pranks. If bicycle riders were struck by mango seeds or apricot stones, they would look up, see a small boy in the branches of the tree, and threaten me with terrible consequences. Drivers who went off after parking their cars in the shade would sometimes come back to find their tyres flat. My protests of innocence did not carry much weight. But when I mentioned the pret in the tree, they would look uneasy, either because they thought I must be mad, or because they were afraid of ghosts, especially prets. They would find other things to do and hurry away.

At night no one walked beneath the peepul tree.

It was said that if you yawned beneath the tree, the pret would jump down your throat and give you a pain. Our gardener, Chandu, who was always taking sick leave, blamed the pret for his tummy troubles. Once, when yawning, Chandu had forgotten to put his hand in front of his mouth, and the ghost had got in without any trouble.

Now Chandu spent most of his time lying on a string-bed in the courtyard of his small house. When Grandmother went to visit him, he would start groaning and holding his sides, the pain was so bad; but when she went away, he did not fuss so much. He claimed that the pain did not affect his appetite, and he ate a normal diet, in fact a little more than normal—the extra amount was meant to keep the ghost happy!

II

'Well, it isn't our fault,' said Grandfather, who had given permission to the Public Works Department to cut the tree, which had been on our land. They wanted to widen the road, and the tree and a bit of our wall were in the way. So both had to go.

Several people protested, including the Raja of Jinn, who lived across the road and who sometimes asked Grandfather over for a game of tennis.

'That peepul tree has been there for hundreds of years,' he said. 'Who are we to cut it down?'

'We,' said the chief engineer, 'are the P. W. D.'

And not even a ghost can prevail against the wishes of the Public Works Department.

They brought men with saws and axes, and first they lopped all the branches until the poor tree was quite naked. It must have been at this moment that the pret moved out. Then they sawed away at the trunk until, finally, the great old peepul came crashing down on the road, bringing down the telephone wires and an electric pole in the process, and knocking a large gap in the raja's garden wall.

It took them three days to clear the road, and during that time the chief engineer swallowed a lot of dust and tree pollen. For months afterwards he complained of a choking feeling, although no doctor could ever find anything in his throat.

'It's the pret's doing,' said the raja knowingly. 'They should never have cut that tree.'

⁓

Deprived of his tree, the pret decided that he would live in our house.

I first became aware of his presence when I was sitting on the veranda steps reading a book. A tiny chuckling sound came from behind me. I looked around, but no one was to be seen. When I returned to my book, the chuckling started again. I paid no attention. Then a shower of rose petals fell softly on to the pages of my open book. The pret wanted me to know he was there!

'All right,' I said. 'So you've come to stay with us. Now let me read.'

He went away then; but as a good pret has to be bad in order to justify his existence, it was not long before he was up to all sorts of mischief.

He began by hiding Grandmother's spectacles.

'I'm sure I put them down on the dining table,' she grumbled.

A little later they were found balanced on the snout

of a wild boar, whose stuffed and mounted head adorned the veranda wall, a memento of Grandfather's hunting trips when he was young.

Naturally, I was at first blamed for this prank. But a day or two later, when the spectacles disappeared again, only to be found dangling from the bars of the parrot's cage, it was agreed that I was not to blame; for the parrot had once bitten off a piece of my finger, and I did not go near him any more.

The parrot was hanging upside down, trying to peer through one of the lenses. I don't know if they improved his vision, but what he saw certainly made him angry, because the pupils of his eyes went very small and he dug his beak into the spectacle frames, leaving them with a permanent dent. I caught them just before they fell to the floor.

But even without the help of the spectacles, it seemed that our parrot could see the pret. He would keep turning this way and that, lunging out at unseen fingers, and protecting his tail from the tweaks of invisible hands. He had always refused to learn to talk, but now he became quite voluble and began to chatter in some unknown tongue, often screaming with rage and rolling his eyes in a frenzy.

'We'll have to give that parrot away,' said Grandmother.

'He gets more bad-tempered by the day.'

Grandfather was the next to be troubled. He went into the garden one morning to find all his prize sweet peas broken off and lying on the grass. Chandu thought the sparrows had destroyed the flowers, but we didn't think the birds could have finished off every single bloom just before sunrise.

'It must be the pret,' said Grandfather, and I agreed.

The pret did not trouble me much, because he remembered me from his peepul tree days and knew I resented the tree being cut as much as he did. But he liked to catch my attention, and he did this by chuckling and squeaking near me when I was alone, or whispering in my ear when I was with someone else. Gradually I began to make out the occasional word. He had started learning English!

III

Uncle Benji, who came to stay with us for long periods when he had little else to do (which was most of the time), was soon to suffer.

He was a heavy sleeper, and once he'd gone to bed he hated being woken up. So when he came to breakfast looking bleary-eyed and miserable, we asked him if he was feeling all right.

'I couldn't sleep a wink last night,' he complained. 'Whenever I was about to fall asleep, the bedclothes would be pulled off the bed. I had to get up at least a dozen times to pick them off the floor.' He stared suspiciously at me. 'Where were *you* sleeping last night, young man?'

'In Grandfather's room,' I said. 'I've lent you *my* room.'

'It's that ghost from the peepul tree,' said Grandmother with a sigh.

'Ghost!' exclaimed Uncle Benji. 'I didn't know the house was haunted.'

'It is now,' said Grandmother. 'First, my spectacles, then the sweet peas, and now Benji's bedclothes! What will it be up to next, I wonder?'

We did not have to wonder for long.

There followed a series of minor disasters. Vases fell off tables, pictures fell from walls. Parrot feathers turned up in the teapot, while the parrot himself let out indignant squawks and swear words in the middle of the night. Windows which had been closed would be found open, and open windows closed.

Finally, Uncle Benji found a crow's nest in his bed, and on tossing it out of the window was attacked by two crows.

Then Aunt Ruby came to stay, and things quietened down for a time.

Did Aunt Ruby's powerful personality have an effect on the pret, or was he just sizing her up?

'I think the pret has taken a fancy to your aunt,' said Grandfather mischievously. 'He's behaving himself for a change.'

This may have been true, because the parrot, who had picked up some of the English words being tried out by the pret, now called out, '*kiss,*' whenever Aunt Ruby was in the room.

'What a charming bird,' said Aunt Ruby.

'You can keep him if you like,' said Grandmother.

One day Aunt Ruby came into the house covered in rose petals.

'I don't know where they came from,' she exclaimed. 'I was sitting in the garden, drying my hair, when handfuls of petals came showering down on me!'

'He likes you,' said Grandfather.

'Who likes me?'

'The ghost.'

'What ghost?'

'The pret. He came to live in the house when the peepul tree was cut down.'

'What nonsense!' said Aunt Ruby.

'*Kiss, kiss!*' screamed the parrot.

'There aren't any ghosts, prets or other kinds,' said

Aunt Ruby firmly.

'*Kiss, kiss!*' screeched the parrot again. Or was it the pret? The sound seemed to be coming from the ceiling.

'I wish that parrot would shut up.'

'It isn't the parrot,' I said. 'It's the pret.'

Aunt Ruby gave me a cuff over the ear and stormed out of the room.

But she had offended the pret. From being her admirer, he turned into her enemy. Somehow her toothpaste got switched with a tube of Grandfather's shaving cream. When she appeared in the dining room, foaming at the mouth, we ran for our lives, Uncle Benji shouting that she'd got rabies.

IV

Two days later Aunt Ruby complained that she had been struck on the nose by a grapefruit, which had leapt mysteriously from the pantry shelf and hurled itself at her.

'If Ruby and Benji stay here much longer, they'll both have nervous breakdowns,' said Grandfather thoughtfully.

'I thought they broke down long ago,' I said.

'None of your cheek,' snapped Aunt Ruby.

'He's in league with that pret to try and get us out

The Shadow on the Wall

of here,' said Uncle Benji.

'Don't listen to him—you can stay as long as you like,' said Grandmother, who never turned away any of her numerous nephews, nieces, cousins, or distant relatives.

The pret, however, did not feel so hospitable, and the persecution of Aunt Ruby continued.

'When I looked in the mirror this morning,' she complained bitterly, 'I saw a little monster, with huge ears, bulging eyes, flaring nostrils, and a toothless grin!'

'You don't look that bad, Aunt Ruby,' I said, trying to be nice.

'It was either you or that imp you call a pret,' said Aunt Ruby. 'And if it's a ghost, then it's time we all moved to another house.'

Uncle Benji had another idea.

'Let's drive the ghost out,' he said. 'I know a sadhu who rids houses of evil spirits.'

'But the pret's not evil,' I said. 'Just mischievous.'

Uncle Benji went off to the bazaar and came back a few hours later with a mysterious, long-haired man who claimed to be a sadhu—one who has given up all worldly goods, including most of his clothes.

He prowled about the house, and lighted incense in all the rooms, despite squawks of protest from the parrot. All the time he chanted various magic spells. He then collected a fee of thirty rupees, and promised that we would not be bothered again by the pret.

As he was leaving, he was suddenly blessed with a shower—no, it was really a downpour—of dead flowers, decaying leaves, orange peel, and banana skins. All spells forgotten, he ran to the gate and made for the safety of the bazaar.

Aunt Ruby declared that it had become impossible to sleep at night because of the devilish chuckling that came from beneath her pillow. She packed her bags and left.

Uncle Benji stayed on. He was still having trouble with his bedclothes, and he was beginning to talk to himself, which was a bad sign.

'Talking to the pret, Uncle?' I asked innocently, when I caught him at it one day.

He gave me a threatening look. 'What did you say?' he demanded. 'Would you mind repeating that?'

I thought it safer to please him. 'Oh, didn't you hear me? I said, "Teaching the parrot, Uncle?"'

He glared at me, then walked off in a huff. If he did not leave it was because he was hoping Grandmother would lend him enough money to buy a motorcycle; but

The Shadow on the Wall

Grandmother said he ought to try earning a living first.

One day I found him on the drawing room sofa, laughing like a madman. Even the parrot was so alarmed that he was silent, head lowered and curious. Uncle Benji was red in the face—literally red all over!

'What happened to your face, Uncle?' I asked. He stopped laughing and gave me a long, hard look. I realized that there had been no joy in his laughter.

'Who painted the washbasin red without telling me?' he asked in a quavering voice.

As Uncle Benji looked really dangerous, I ran from the room.

'We'll have to move, I suppose,' said Grandfather later.

'Even if it's only for a couple of months, I'm worried about Benji. I've told him that I painted the washbasin myself but forgot to tell him. He doesn't believe me. He thinks it's the pret or the boy or both of them! Benji needs a change. So do we. There's my brother's house at the other end of the town. He won't be using it for a few months. We'll move in next week.'

And so, a few days and several disasters later, we began moving house.

V

Two bullock carts laden with furniture and heavy luggage were sent ahead. Uncle Benji went with them. The roof of our old car was piled high with bags and kitchen utensils. Grandfather took the wheel, I sat beside him, and Granny sat in state at the back.

We set off and had gone some way down the main road when Grandfather started having trouble with the steering wheel. It appeared to have got loose, and the car began veering about on the road, scattering cyclists, pedestrians, and stray dogs, pigs, and hens. A cow refused to move, but we missed it somehow, and then suddenly we were off the road and making for a low wall. Grandfather pressed his foot down on the brake, but we only went faster. 'Watch out!' he shouted.

It was the Raja of Jinn's garden wall, made of single bricks, and the car knocked it down quite easily and went on through it, coming to a stop on the raja's lawn.

'Now look what you've done,' said Grandmother.

'Well, we missed the flower beds,' said Grandfather.

'Someone's been tinkering with the car. Our pret, no doubt.'

The raja and two attendants came running towards us.

The raja was a perfect gentleman, and when he saw that the driver was Grandfather, he beamed with pleasure.

'Delighted to see you, old chap!' he exclaimed. 'Jolly decent of you to drop in. How about a game of tennis?'

'Sorry to have come in through the wall,' apologized Grandfather.

'Don't mention it, old chap. The gate was closed, so what else could you do?'

Grandfather was as much of a gentleman as the raja, so he thought it only fair to join him in a game of tennis. Grandmother and I watched and drank lemonade. After the game, the raja waved us goodbye and we drove back through the hole in the wall and out on to the road. There was nothing much wrong with the car.

We hadn't gone far when we heard a peculiar sound, as of someone chuckling and talking to himself. It came from the roof of the car.

'Is the parrot out there on the luggage rack?' asked Grandfather.

'No,' said Grandmother. 'He went ahead with Uncle Benji.'

Grandfather stopped the car, got out, and examined the roof. 'Nothing up there,' he said, getting in again and starting the engine. 'I thought I heard the parrot.'

When we had gone a little further, the chuckling started again. A squeaky little voice began talking in English in the tones of the parrot.

'It's the pret,' whispered Grandmother. 'What is he saying?'

The pret's squeak grew louder. 'Come on, come on!' he cried gleefully. 'A new house! The same old friends! What fun we're going to have!'

Grandfather stopped the car. He backed into a driveway, turned around, and began driving back to our old house.

'What are you doing?' asked Grandmother.

'Going home,' said Grandfather.

'And what about the pret?'

'What about him? He's decided to live with us, so we'll have to make the best of it. You can't solve a problem by running away from it.'

'All right,' said Grandmother. 'But what will we do about Benji?'

'It's up to him, isn't it? He'll be all right if he finds something to do.'

Grandfather stopped the car in front of the veranda steps.

'I'm hungry,' I said.

'It will have to be a picnic lunch,' said Grandmother. 'Almost everything was sent off on the bullock carts.'

As we got out of the car and climbed the veranda

steps, we were greeted by showers of rose petals and sweet-scented jasmine.

'How lovely!' exclaimed Grandmother, smiling. 'I think he likes us, after all.'

THE DOPPELGÄNGER

It was in 1960, or thereabouts, that I first met a doppelgänger.

There, I have at least spelt it right. It's a German word but you can find it in the *Oxford Dictionary of English*, where so many exotic words turn up.

I was twenty-six at the time. I'd had a novel published in London, but very few people bought it, and my freelancing efforts in New Delhi were appreciated but seldom rewarded. I had taken a job with CARE, an American relief agency, and they sent me to Darjeeling (among other places) to see what help could be given to the Tibetan refugees who had arrived there.

So I was a nobody, trying to be a somebody.

When I entered the portals of the old Everest Hotel,

I found it full of somebodys. There was Shammi Kapoor and his Bollywood crew, engaged in making a romantic film called *Professor*. And there was Satyajit Ray and his crew from Kolkata, engaged in making an artistic film called *Kanchenjunga*.

Kanchenjunga was the name of the majestic peak visible from Darjeeling, and while I was there I had a glimpse of it as well as a few glimpses of the shooting of these two contrasting films. But this is not the story of those films, or of my work with the Tibetans, but of an encounter that took place because of them.

Free one afternoon, I was strolling along the Darjeeling Mall when I heard a stentorious voice call out, 'Mr Bond! Have you got my Henry Green?'

It was Marie Seton.

I had met Marie Seton a few times in New Delhi, having been introduced to her by the chief of CARE, who had written a book about Laos. Marie was much older than me, but she was good company, and we would often meet at the India Coffee House and have long, gossipy chats over a pot of strong coffee. She was a film enthusiast, had edited Eisenstein's unfinished *Que Viva Mexico*, which I had seen in London, and was now engaged in writing the filmography of Satyajit Ray's films. That accounted for her presence in Darjeeling.

The Doppelgänger

'Your Henry Green?' I countered, as we came face to face, 'I have never read Henry Green.' He was an author who was currently in fashion, but I had yet to meet someone who had read his works.

'I am sure I lent it to you,' she said vaguely. 'Or maybe it was to Khushwant. Anyway what are you doing up here? You're not with that lot from Bombay, are you—singing and dancing on the railway tracks?'

'No, of course not.' But I felt a little guilty, because only that morning I had exchanged a few words with the charming Geeta Bali, Mr Kapoor's wife. She was not in the film—had retired from filming because of poor health—but was still very attractive in her own unique way.

'I can't sing and I can't dance,' I said. 'But come and have a coffee, and I'll tell you why I am here.'

So we sat at the wayside café and chatted about books and films and the British royal family (she was an expert on the royal family and knew all of them, apparently), and even promised to introduce me to the great Satyajit Ray later that evening.

And so we parted, and I went about my work, returning to the hotel at about six in the evening. The lobby was full of all the film people, but there was no sign of Marie Seton, and when I enquired at the reception I was told that no one by that name was staying there.

Never mind. She must've been staying somewhere else, in a more modest hotel, and presumably at her own expense. I went for a long walk in Darjeeling's December mist, and forgot all about our encounter.

A few weeks later I was back in New Delhi, strolling around Connaught Place in search of a bookshop, when I heard that familiar voice. 'What have you done with my Henry Green?'

It was Marie Seton again.

'You know I don't have it,' I protested. 'I haven't read Henry Green and have no desire to read his damn book. So come and have a coffee and bring me up to date on all the royal gossip.'

We went into Nirula's and caught up with each other's news.

'So tell me,' I asked, 'how did the shooting go in Darjeeling? We were supposed to meet, but I couldn't find you at the hotel—'

'What hotel? What are you talking about?'

'Last month in Darjeeling. Don't you remember? We met on the Mall, while Ray was filming *Kanchenjunga*.'

'My dear boy, I've never been to Darjeeling. You've been imagining things—reading too much Anaïs Nin! I wish I'd been there, though. Watching Ray at work—just what I need for my book. But it was not to be. I was down with flu at the time.'

'But you were there—we met on the Mall—you asked me for your wretched Henry Green!'

'Nonsense! I couldn't have been in two places at once.'

And then it occurred to me—perhaps she was a doppelgänger, capable of being in two places at once! I gave a little shudder. Somehow a doppelgänger was scarier than a ghost; a living person with supernatural qualities. Was she, even now, real? Or was she just an apparition sipping coffee with me? Of course she had been in Darjeeling that day. And perhaps she was somewhere else, even now. She could be having tea at Buckingham Palace! No wonder she was so well-informed on royalty....

I got up to leave; made some lame excuse about a prior appointment; promised to meet her again.

'Farewell, dear boy,' she said with a sinister smile. 'And don't forget my Henry Green.'

∾

Well, I had yet to come across a copy of a Henry Green novel, although I know that such a writer did exist; forgotten, if he was ever remembered. And I did not see Marie Seton again for a couple of years, although I felt sure she was doppelgänging all over the place.

The Shadow on the Wall

And then one day I was at the New Delhi railway station, accompanied by a young writer called Sasthi Brata, who was to make a name for himself with a confessional novel called *My God Died Young*. We were seeing off Professor P. Lal, an academic whose Writers Workshop in Kolkata was the last resort for many an aspiring writer.

We had paid our respects to the great man, and the train was beginning to move, when I caught sight of Marie Seton in the next compartment. She was reading a book. I called out to her, and she looked up, but I don't think she saw me, as just then the train picked up speed, and her compartment swept past me.

'Who did you call out to?' asked my companion.

'Marie Seton,' I said. 'She's always turning up in unexpected places.'

'It couldn't have been her,' said Sasthi B. 'She died on a film set in Bhutan about two months ago.'

'It was Marie Seton in that carriage,' I insisted.

'Then you saw her ghost,' he said. 'Or someone who looked just like her.'

So now even her ghost was a doppelgänger!

I gave up. And when I got home to my room in East Patel Nagar I wasn't a bit surprised to find a Henry Green novel on my desk.

While rounding of this little tale it has occurred to me

that everyone mentioned in it—writers, actors, directors, singers, academics—have all made their exits from life on this particular planet and have, hopefully, moved on to a better place—or to complete nothingness—leaving behind some memorials to their artistry: books, films, songs, poems, creative contributions big or small to the passing show.

There is a Latin proverb—

Ars longa, vita brevis...

Art is long life is short.

Or, to turn it around: life is short, but art is long.

THE WIND ON HAUNTED HILL

Whoo, whoo, whoo, cried the wind as it swept down from the Himalayan snows. It hurried over the hills and passed and hummed and moaned through the tall pines and deodars. There was little on Haunted Hill to stop the wind—only a few stunted trees and bushes and the ruins of a small settlement.

On the slopes of the next hill was a village. People kept large stones on their tin roofs to prevent them from being blown off. There was nearly always a strong wind in these parts. Three children were spreading clothes out to dry on a low stone wall, putting a stone on each piece.

Eleven-year-old Usha, dark-haired and rose-cheeked, struggled with her grandfather's long, loose shirt. Her younger brother, Suresh, was doing his best to hold down a bedsheet, while Usha's friend, Binya, a slightly older girl, helped.

Once everything was firmly held down by stones, they climbed up on the flat rocks and sat there sunbathing and staring across the fields at the ruins on Haunted Hill.

'I must go to the bazaar today,' said Usha.

'I wish I could come too,' said Binya. 'But I have to help with the cows.'

'I can come!' said eight-year-old Suresh. He was always ready to visit the bazaar, which was three miles away, on the other side of the hill.

'No, you can't,' said Usha. 'You must help Grandfather chop wood.'

'Won't you feel scared returning alone?' he asked. 'There are ghosts on Haunted Hill!'

'I'll be back before dark. Ghosts don't appear during the day.'

'Are there lots of ghosts in the ruins?' asked Binya.

'Grandfather says so. He says that over a hundred years ago, some Britishers lived on the hill. But the settlement was always being struck by lightning, so they moved away.'

'But if they left, why is the place visited by ghosts?'

'Because—Grandfather says—during a terrible storm, one of the houses was hit by lightning, and everyone in it was killed. Even the children.'

'How many children?'

'Two. A boy and his sister. Grandfather saw them playing there in the moonlight.'

'Wasn't he frightened?'

'No. Old people don't mind ghosts.'

Usha set out for the bazaar at two in the afternoon. It was about an hour's walk. The path went through yellow fields of flowering mustard, then along the saddle of the hill, and up, straight through the ruins. Usha had often gone that way to shop at the bazaar or to see her aunt, who lived in the town nearby.

Wild flowers bloomed on the crumbling walls of the ruins, and a wild plum tree grew straight out of the floor of what had once been a hall. It was covered with soft, white blossoms. Lizards scuttled over the stones, while a whistling thrush, its deep purple plumage glistening in the sunshine, sat on a windowsill and sang its heart out.

Usha sang too, as she skipped lightly along the path, which dipped steeply down to the valley and led to the little town with its quaint bazaar.

Moving leisurely, Usha bought spices, sugar, and matches. With the two rupees she had saved from her pocket money, she chose a necklace of amber-coloured beads for herself and some marbles for Suresh. Then she had her mother's slippers repaired at a cobbler's shop.

Finally, Usha went to visit Aunt Lakshmi at her flat above the shops. They were talking and drinking cups of hot, sweet tea when Usha realized that dark clouds had gathered over the mountains. She quickly picked up her things, said goodbye to her aunt, and set out for the village.

Strangely, the wind had dropped. The trees were still, the crickets silent. The crows flew round in circles, then settled on an oak tree.

'I must get home before dark,' thought Usha, hurrying along the path.

But the sky had darkened and a deep rumble echoed over the hills. Usha felt the first heavy drop of rain hit her cheek. Holding the shopping bag close to her body, she quickened her pace until she was almost running. The raindrops were coming down faster now—cold, stinging pellets of rain. A flash of lightning sharply outlined the ruins on the hill, and then all was dark again. Night had fallen.

'I'll have to shelter in the ruins,' Usha thought and began to run. Suddenly the wind sprang up again, but she did not have to fight it. It was behind her now, helping her along, up the steep path and on to the brow of the hill. There was another flash of lightning, followed by a peal of thunder. The ruins loomed before her, grim and forbidding.

Usha remembered part of an old roof that would give some shelter. It would be better than trying to go on. In the dark, with the howling wind, she might stray off the path and fall over the edge of the cliff.

Whoo, whoo, whoo, howled the wind. Usha saw the wild plum tree swaying, its foliage thrashing against the ground. She found her way into the ruins, helped by the constant flicker of lightning. Usha placed her hands flat against a stone wall and moved sideways, hoping to reach the sheltered corner. Suddenly, her hand touched something soft and furry, and she gave a startled cry. Her cry was answered by another—half snarl, half screech—as something leapt away in the darkness.

With a sigh of relief Usha realized that it was the cat that lived in the ruins. For a moment she had been frightened, but now she moved quickly along the wall until she heard the rain drumming on a remnant of a tin roof. Crouched in a corner, she found some shelter. But the tin sheet groaned and clattered as if it would sail away any moment.

Usha remembered that across this empty room stood an old fireplace. Perhaps it would be drier there under the blocked chimney. But she would not attempt to find it just now—she might lose her way altogether.

Her clothes were soaked and water streamed down

from her hair, forming a puddle at her feet. She thought she heard a faint cry—the cat again, or an owl? Then the storm blotted out all other sounds.

There had been no time to think of ghosts, but now that she was settled in one place, Usha remembered Grandfather's story about the lightning-blasted ruins. She hoped and prayed that lightning would not strike her.

Thunder boomed over the hills, and the lightning came quicker now. Then there was a bigger flash, and for a moment the entire ruin was lit up. A streak of blue sizzled along the floor of the building. Usha was staring straight ahead, and, as the opposite wall lit up, she saw, crouching in front of the unused fireplace, two small figures—children!

The ghostly figures seemed to look up and stare back at Usha. And then everything was dark again.

Usha's heart was in her mouth. She had seen without doubt, two ghosts on the other side of the room. She wasn't going to remain in the ruins one minute longer.

She ran towards the big gap in the wall through which she had entered. She was halfway across the open space when something—someone—fell against her. Usha stumbled, got up, and again bumped into something. She gave a frightened scream. Someone else screamed. And then there was a shout, a boy's shout, and Usha instantly recognized the voice.

'Suresh!'

'Usha!'

'Binya!'

They fell into each other's arms, so surprised and relieved that all they could do was laugh and giggle and repeat each other's names.

Then Usha said, 'I thought you were ghosts.'

'We thought you were a ghost,' said Suresh.

'Come back under the roof,' said Usha.

They huddled together in the corner, chattering with excitement and relief.

'When it grew dark, we came looking for you,' said Binya. 'And then the storm broke.'

'Shall we run back together?' asked Usha. 'I don't want to stay here any longer.'

'We'll have to wait,' said Binya. 'The path has fallen away at one place. It won't be safe in the dark, in all this rain.'

'We'll have to wait till morning,' said Suresh, 'and I'm so hungry!'

The storm continued, but they were not afraid now. They gave each other warmth and confidence. Even the ruins did not seem so forbidding.

After an hour the rain stopped, and the thunder grew more distant.

Towards dawn the whistling thrush began to sing. Its sweet, broken notes flooded the ruins with music. As the sky grew lighter, they saw that the plum tree stood upright again, though it had lost all its blossoms.

'Let's go,' said Usha.

Outside the ruins, walking along the brow of the hill, they watched the sky grow pink. When they were some distance away, Usha looked back and said, 'Can you see something behind the wall? It's like a hand waving.'

'It's just the top of the plum tree,' said Binya.

'Goodbye, goodbye...' They heard voices.

'Who said "goodbye"?' asked Usha.

'Not I,' said Suresh.

'Nor I,' said Binya.

'I heard someone calling,' said Usha.

'It's only the wind,' assured Binya.

Usha looked back at the ruins. The sun had come up and was touching the top of the wall.

'Come on,' said Suresh. 'I'm hungry.'

They hurried along the path to the village.

'Goodbye, goodbye...' Usha heard them calling. Or was it just the wind?

WELCOME, GOOD SPIRITS!

The British left India in 1947, but they left their ghosts behind. In old dak bungalows across the country, in forest rest houses, in hill stations, in cantonment towns and seaside resorts, the traveller might well encounter the resident spirit of a former sahib or memsahib determined to 'stay on, in spirit if not in the flesh'.

I live in Landour, the cantonment area just above Mussoorie, and most of the houses on the hillside were built well over a hundred years ago. In fact, some of them go back to the founding of this hill station in the 1820s. The old cemetery, facing the eternal snows, provided shelter to the graves of the many soldiers and officers who were brought to this convalescent depot, in order to recuperate from wounds or illnesses. Not everyone recovered. Families came up too, to get away from the heat and dust of the plains, but infant mortality was high, even in hill stations. The graves of mothers and small children dot the hillside.

You are unlikely to encounter a ghost during a walk past the cemetery, but some of the old houses are reputed to be haunted. Not so long ago, on an early morning walk, I met a family from Delhi hurriedly vacating a guest house, complaining that they had been kept up all night by the visitations of a weeping lady who was wandering about in search of a lost child. Afraid that she might make off with one of their children, they quit the place in a hurry.

I live in a very old house, and although I am not prone to seeing ghosts, I do hear them occasionally.

Late at night, I hear desultory conversations taking place in the sitting room which adjoins my bedroom. No one sleeps there. Rakesh and Beena have their room at the other end of the flat. But the conversations go on for some time, becoming quite lively as the night progresses. I can't make out what is being said, but a party appears to be in progress, perhaps a Christmas party from long, long ago, their talk and laughter trapped in the warp of time.

One night, feeling hungry myself, I got up and went into the front room, switching on all the lights. There was no one there. When I returned to my room, the party began again! It must have been a very exclusive party, if they didn't want me butting in.

But they must have relented and felt sorry for me. This morning, as I opened my doors to the early December sunshine, I found a large Christmas plum pudding on the table in my front room. There was no card or note beside it. How did it get there and that too with all the doors closed? Did my spooky late night visitants leave it there for me? I decided to taste some of it—just in case it was over a hundred years old.

Well, it's a perfectly good pudding. Just the right amount of brandy in it. I think I'll have another slice. And if my ghostly partygoers are here again tonight, I won't complain.

THE WHISTLING SCHOOLBOY

The moon was almost at the full. Bright moonlight flooded the road. But I was stalked by the shadows of the trees, by the crooked oak branches reaching out towards me—some threateningly, others as though they needed companionship.

Once I dreamt that the trees could walk. That on moonlit nights like this they would uproot themselves for a while, visit each other, talk about old times—for they had seen many men and happenings, especially the older ones. And then, before dawn, they would return to the places where they had been condemned to grow. Lonely sentinels of the night. And this was a good night for them to walk. They appeared eager to do so: a restless rustling of leaves, the creaking of branches—these were sounds that came from within them in the silence of the night.

Occasionally other strollers passed me in the dark. It was still quite early, just eight o'clock, and some people were on their way home. Others were walking into town for a taste of the bright lights, shops, and restaurants. On the unlit road I could not recognize them. They did not notice me. I was reminded of an old song from my childhood. Softly, I began humming the tune, and soon the words came back to me:

We three, We're not a crowd; We're not even company—
My echo, My shadow, And me...

I looked down at my shadow, moving silently beside me. We take our shadows for granted, don't we? There they are, the uncomplaining companions of a lifetime, mute and helpless witnesses to our every act of commission or omission. On this bright moonlit night I could not help noticing you, Shadow, and I was sorry that you had to see so much that I was ashamed of; but glad, too, that you were around when I had my small triumphs. And what of my echo? I thought of calling out to see if my call came back to me; but I refrained from doing so, as I did not wish to disturb the perfect stillness of the mountains or the conversations of the trees.

The road wound up the hill and levelled out at the

top, where it became a ribbon of moonlight entwined between tall deodars. A flying squirrel glided across the road, leaving one tree for another. A nightjar called. The rest was silence.

The old cemetery loomed up before me. There were many old graves—some large and monumental—and there were a few recent graves too, for the cemetery was still in use. I could see flowers scattered on one of them—a few late dahlias and scarlet salvia. Further on near the boundary wall, part of the cemetery's retaining wall had collapsed in the heavy monsoon rains. Some of the tombstones had come down with the wall. One grave lay exposed. A rotting coffin and a few scattered bones were the only relics of someone who had lived and loved like you and me.

Part of the tombstone lay beside the road, but the lettering had worn away. I am not normally a morbid person, but something made me stoop and pick up a smooth, round shard of bone, probably part of a skull. When my hand closed over it, the bone crumbled into fragments. I let them fall to the grass. Dust to dust. And from somewhere, not too far away, came the sound of someone whistling.

At first I thought it was another late evening stroller, whistling to himself much as I had been humming my old song. But the whistler approached quite rapidly; the whistling was loud and cheerful. A boy on a bicycle sped past. I had only a glimpse of him, before his cycle went weaving through the shadows on the road.

But he was back again in a few minutes. And this time he stopped a few feet away from me, and gave me a quizzical half-smile. A slim dusky boy of fourteen or fifteen. He wore a school blazer and a yellow scarf. His eyes were pools of liquid moonlight.

'You don't have a bell on your cycle,' I said.

He said nothing, just smiled at me with his head a little to one side. I put out my hand, and I thought he was going to take it. But then, quite suddenly, he was off again, whistling cheerfully though rather tunelessly. A whistling schoolboy. A bit late for him to be out but he seemed an independent sort.

The whistling grew fainter, then faded away altogether. A deep, sound-denying silence fell upon the forest. My shadow and I walked home.

Next morning I woke to a different kind of whistling—the song of the thrush outside my window.

It was a wonderful day, the sunshine warm and sensuous, and I longed to be out in the open. But there was work to be done, proofs to be corrected, letters to be written. And it was several days before I could walk to the top of the hill, to that lonely, tranquil resting place under the deodars. It seemed to me ironic that those who had the best view of the glistening, snow-capped peaks were all buried several feet underground.

Some repair work was going on. The retaining wall of the cemetery was being shored up, but the overseer told me that there was no money to restore the damaged grave. With the help of the chowkidar, I returned the scattered bones to a little hollow under the collapsed masonry, and left some money with him so that he could have the open grave bricked up. The name on the gravestone had worn away, but I could make out a date—20 November 1950—some fifty years ago, but not too long ago as gravestones go.

I found the burial register in the church vestry and turned back the yellowing pages to 1950, when I was just a schoolboy myself. I found the name there—Michael Dutta, aged fifteen—and the cause of death: road accident.

Well, I could only make guesses. And to turn conjecture into certainty, I would have to find an old resident who might remember the boy or the accident.

There was old Miss Marley at Pine Top. A retired teacher from Woodstock, she had a wonderful memory, and had lived in the hill station for more than half a century.

White-haired and smooth-cheeked, her bright blue eyes full of curiosity, she gazed benignly at me through her old-fashioned pince-nez.

'Michael was a charming boy—full of exuberance, always ready to oblige. I had only to mention that I needed a newspaper or an aspirin, and he'd be off on his bicycle, swooping down these steep roads with great abandon. But these hill roads, with their sudden corners, weren't meant for racing around on a bicycle. They were widening our roads for motor traffic, and a truck was coming uphill, loaded with rubble, when Michael came round a bend and smashed headlong into it. He was rushed to the hospital, and the doctors did their best, but he did not recover consciousness. Of course, you must have seen his grave. That's why you're here. His parents? They left shortly afterwards. Went abroad, I think.... A charming boy, Michael, but just a bit too reckless. You'd have liked him, I think.'

I did not see the phantom bicycle rider again for some time, although I felt his presence on more than one occasion. And when, on a cold winter's evening, I walked past that lonely cemetery, I thought I heard him whistling far away. But he did not manifest himself. Perhaps it was only the echo of a whistle, in communion with my insubstantial shadow.

It was several months before I saw that smiling face again. And then it came at me out of the mist as I was walking home in drenching monsoon rain. I had been to a dinner party at the old community centre, and I was returning home along a very narrow, precipitous path known as the Eyebrow. A storm had been threatening all evening. A heavy mist had settled on the hillside. It was so thick that the light from my torch simply bounced off it. The sky blossomed with sheet lightning and thunder rolled over the mountains. The rain became heavier. I moved forward slowly, carefully, hugging the hillside. There was a clap of thunder, and then I saw him emerge from the mist and stand in my way—the same slim dark youth who had materialized near the cemetery. He did not smile. Instead he put up his hand and waved at me. I hesitated, stood still. The mist lifted a little, and I saw that the path had disappeared. There was a gaping emptiness a few feet in front of me. And then a drop of over a hundred feet to the rocks below.

As I stepped back, clinging to a thorn bush for support, the boy vanished. I stumbled back to the community centre and spent the night on a chair in the library.

I did not see him again.

But weeks later, when I was down with a severe bout of flu, I heard him from my sickbed, whistling beneath my window. Was he calling to me to join him, I wondered, or was he just trying to reassure me that all was well? I got out of bed and looked out, but I saw no one. From time to time I heard his whistling; but, as I got better, it grew fainter until it ceased altogether.

Fully recovered, I renewed my old walks to the top of the hill. But although I lingered near the cemetery until it grew dark, and paced up and down the deserted road, I did not see or hear the whistler again. I felt lonely, in need of a friend, even if it was only a phantom bicycle rider. But there were only the trees.

And so every evening I walk home in the darkness, singing the old refrain:

We three, We're not a crowd; We're not even company—
My echo, My shadow, And me...

SOME HILL STATION GHOSTS

Shimla has its phantom rickshaw and Lansdowne its headless horseman. Mussoorie has its woman in white. Late at night, she can be seen sitting on the parapet wall on the winding road up to the hill station. Don't stop to offer her a lift. She will fix you with her evil eye and ruin your holiday.

The Mussoorie taxi drivers and other locals call her Bhoot-aunty. Everyone has seen her at some time or the other. To give her a lift is to court disaster. Many accidents have been attributed to her baleful presence. And when people pick themselves up from the road (or are picked up by concerned citizens), Bhoot-aunty is nowhere to be seen, although survivors swear that she was in the car with them.

Ganesh Saili, Abha and I were coming back from Dehradun late one night when we saw this woman in white sitting on the parapet by the side of the road. As our headlights fell on her, she turned her face away, Ganesh, being a thorough gentleman, slowed down and offered her a lift. She turned towards us then, and smiled a wicked smile. She seemed quite attractive except that her canines protruded slightly in vampire fashion.

'Don't stop!' screamed Abha. 'Don't even look at her! It's Bhoot-aunty!'

Ganesh pressed down on the accelerator and sped past her. Next day we heard that a tourist's car had gone off the road and the occupants had been severely injured. The accident took place shortly after they had stopped to pick up a woman in white who had wanted a lift. But she was not among the injured.

༄

Miss Ripley-Bean, an old English lady who was my neighbour when I lived near Wynberg-Allen school, told me that her family was haunted by a malignant phantom head that always appeared before the death of one of her relatives.

She said her brother saw this apparition the night

before her mother died, and both she and her sister saw it before the death of their father. The sister slept in the same room. They were both awakened one night by a curious noise in the cupboard facing their beds. One of them began getting out of bed to see if their cat was in the room, when the cupboard door suddenly opened and a luminous head appeared. It was covered with matted hair and appeared to be in an advanced stage of decomposition. Its fleshless mouth grinned at the terrified sisters. And then as they crossed themselves, it vanished. The next day they learned that their father, who was in Lucknow, had died suddenly, at about the time that they had seen the death's head.

∽

Everyone likes to hear stories about haunted houses; even sceptics will listen to a ghost story, while casting doubts on its veracity.

Rudyard Kipling wrote a number of memorable ghost stories set in India—'The Return of Imray', 'The Phantom Rickshaw', 'The Mark of the Beast', 'At the End of the Passage'—his favorite milieu being the haunted dak bungalow. But it was only after his return to England that he found himself actually having to live in a haunted house. He writes about it in his autobiography, *Something of Myself*.

> The spring of '96 saw us in Torquay, where we found a house for our heads that seemed almost too good to be true. It was large and bright, with big rooms each and all open to the sun, the ground embellished with great trees and the warm land dipping southerly to the clean sea under the Mary Church cliffs. It had been inhabited for thirty years by three old maids.
>
> The revelation came in the shape of a growing depression which enveloped us both—a gathering blackness of mind and sorrow of the heart, that each put down to the new, soft climate and, without telling the other, fought against for long weeks. It was the Feng shui—the Spirit of the house itself—that darkened the sunshine and fell upon us every time we entered, checking the very words on our lips.... We paid forfeit and fled. More than thirty years later we returned down the steep little road to that house, and found, quite unchanged, the same brooding spirit of deep despondency within the rooms.

Again, thirty years later, he returned to this house in his short story, 'The House Surgeon', in which two sisters cannot come to terms with the suicide of a third sister, and brood upon the tragedy day and night until their thoughts saturate every room of the house.

Many years ago, I had a similar experience in a house in Dehradun, in which an elderly English couple had died from neglect and starvation. In 1947, when many European residents were leaving the town and emigrating to the UK, this poverty-stricken old couple, sick and friendless, had been forgotten. Too ill to go out for food or medicine, they had died in their beds, where they were discovered several days later by the landlord's munshi.

The house stood empty for several years. No one wanted to live in it. As a young man, I would sometimes roam about the neglected grounds or explore the cold, bare rooms, now stripped of furniture, doorless and windowless, and I would be assailed by a feeling of deep gloom and depression. Of course I knew what had happened there, and that may have contributed to the effect the place had on me. But when I took a friend, Jai Shankar, through the house, he told me he felt quite sick with apprehension and fear. 'Ruskin, why have you brought me to this awful house?' he said. 'I'm sure it's haunted.' And only then did I tell him about the tragedy that had taken place within its walls.

Today, the house is used as a government office. No

one lives in it at night except for a Gurkha chowkidar, a man of strong nerves who sleeps in the back veranda. The atmosphere of the place doesn't bother him, but he does hear strange sounds in the night. 'Like someone crawling about on the floor above,' he tells me. 'And someone groaning. These old houses are noisy places...'

A morgue is not a noisy place, as a rule. And for a morgue attendant, corpses are silent companions.

Old Mr Jacob, who lives just behind the cottage, was once a morgue attendant for the local mission hospital. In those days it was situated at Sunny Bank, about a hundred metres up the hill from here. One of the outhouses served as the morgue: Mr Jacob begs me not to identify it.

He tells me of a terrifying experience he went through when he was doing night duty at the morgue.

'The body of a young man was found floating in the Aglar River, behind Landour, and was brought to the morgue while I was on night duty. It was placed on the table and covered with a sheet.

'I was quite accustomed to seeing corpses of various kinds and did not mind sharing the same room with them, even after dark. On this occasion a friend had promised to join me, and to pass the time I strolled around the room, whistling a popular tune. I think it was "Danny Boy", if I remember right. My friend was a long time coming, and I soon got tired of whistling and sat down on the bench beside the table. The night was very still, and I began to feel uneasy. My thoughts went to the boy who had drowned and I wondered what he had been like when he was alive. Dead bodies are so impersonal....

'The morgue had no electricity, just a kerosene lamp, and after some time I noticed that the flame was very low. As I was about to turn it up, it suddenly went out. I lit the lamp again, after extending the wick. I returned to the bench, but I had not been sitting there for long when the lamp again went out, and something moved very softly and quietly past me.

'I felt quite sick and faint, and could hear my heart pounding away. The strength had gone out of my legs, otherwise I would have fled from the room. I felt quite weak and helpless, unable even to call out....

'Presently the footsteps came nearer and nearer. Something cold and icy touched one of my hands and felt its way up towards my neck and throat. It was behind me, then it was before me. Then it was over me. I was in the arms of the corpse!

'I must have fainted, because when I woke up I was on the floor, and my friend was trying to revive me. The corpse was back on the table.'

'It may have been a nightmare,' I suggested. 'Or you allowed your imagination to run riot.'

'No,' said Mr Jacobs. 'There were wet, slimy marks on my clothes. And the feet of the corpse matched the wet footprints on the floor.'

After this experience, Mr Jacobs refused to do any more night duty at the morgue.

∽

A CHAKRATA HAUNTING

From Herbertpur near Paonta you can go up to Kalsi, and then up the hill road to Chakrata.

Chakrata is in a security zone, most of it off limits to tourists, which is one reason why it has remained unchanged in 150 years of its existence. This small town's population of 1,500 is the same today as it was in 1947—probably the only town in India that hasn't shown a population increase.

Courtesy a government official, I was fortunate enough to be able to stay in the forest rest house on the outskirts of the town. This is a new building, the old rest house—a little way downhill—having fallen into disuse. The chowkidar told me the old rest house was haunted, and that this was the real reason for its having been abandoned. I was a bit sceptical about this, and asked him what kind of haunting took place in it. He told me that he had himself gone through a frightening experience in the old house, when he had gone there to light a fire for some forest officers who were expected that night. After lighting the fire, he looked round and saw a large black animal, like a wild cat, sitting on the wooden floor and gazing into the fire. 'I called out to it, thinking it was someone's pet. The creature turned, and looked full at me with *eyes that were human,* and a face which was the *face of an ugly woman*. The creature snarled at me, and the snarl became an angry howl. Then it vanished!'

'And what did you do?' I asked.

'I vanished too,' said the chowkidar. I haven't been down to that house again.'

I did not volunteer to sleep in the old house but made myself comfortable in the new one, where I hoped I would not be troubled by any phantom. However, a large rat kept me company, gnawing away at the woodwork of a chest of drawers. Whenever I switched on the light it would be silent, but as soon as the light was off, it would start gnawing away again.

This reminded me of a story old Miss Kellner (of my Dehra childhood) told me, of a young man who was desperately in love with a girl who did not care for him. One day, when he was following her in the street, she turned on him and, pointing to a rat which some boys had just killed, said, 'I'd as soon marry that rat as marry you.' He took her cruel words so much to heart that he pined away and died. After his death the girl was haunted at night by a rat and occasionally she would be bitten. When the family decided to emigrate they travelled down to Bombay in order to embark on a ship sailing for London. The ship had just left the quay, when shouts and screams were heard from the pier. The crowd scattered, and a huge rat with fiery eyes ran down to the end of the quay. It sat there, screaming with rage, then jumped into the water and disappeared. After that (according to Miss Kellner), the girl was not haunted again.

Old dak bungalows and forest rest houses have a reputation for being haunted. And most hill stations have their resident ghosts—and ghost writers! But I will not extend this catalogue of ghostly hauntings and visitations, as I do not want to discourage tourists from visiting Landour and Mussoorie. In some countries, ghosts are an added attraction for tourists. Britain boasts of hundreds of haunted castles and stately homes, and visitors to Romania seek out Transylvania and Dracula's castle. So do we promote Bhoot-aunty as a tourist attraction? Only if she reforms and stops sending vehicles off those hairpin bends that lead to Mussoorie.

THE MAN WHO WAS KIPLING

I was sitting on a bench in the Indian Section of the Victoria and Albert Museum in London, when a tall, stooping, elderly gentleman sat down beside me. I gave him a quick glance, noting his swarthy features, heavy moustache, and horn-rimmed spectacles. There was something familiar and disturbing about his face, and I couldn't resist looking at him again.

I noticed that he was smiling at me.

'Do you recognize me?' he asked, in a soft pleasant voice.

'Well, you do seem familiar,' I said. 'Haven't we met somewhere?'

'Perhaps. But if I seem familiar to you, that is at least something. The trouble these days is that people don't know me any more—I'm a familiar, that's all. Just a name standing for a lot of outmoded ideas.'

A little perplexed, I asked, 'What is it you do?'

'I wrote books once. Poems and tales.... Tell me, whose books do you read?'

'Oh, Maugham, Priestley, Thurber. And among the older lot, Bennett and Wells—' I hesitated, groping for an important name, and I noticed a shadow, a sad shadow, pass across my companion's face.

'Oh, yes, and Kipling,' I said, 'I read a lot of Kipling.'

His face brightened up at once, and the eyes behind the thick-lensed spectacles suddenly came to life.

'I'm Kipling,' he said.

I stared at him in astonishment, and then, realizing that he might perhaps be dangerous, I smiled feebly and said, 'Oh, yes?'

'You probably don't believe me. I'm dead, of course.'

'So I thought.'

'And you don't believe in ghosts?'

'Not as a rule.'

'But you'd have no objection to talking to one, if he came along?'

'I'd have no objection. But how do I know you're Kipling? How do I know you're not an imposter?'

'Listen, then:

> When my heavens were turned to blood,
> When the dark had filled my day,
> Furthest, but most faithful, stood
> That lone star I cast away.
> I had loved myself, and I
> Have not lived and dare not die.

'Once,' he said, gripping me by the arm and looking me straight in the eye. 'Once in life I watched a star; but I whistled, her to go.'

'Your star hasn't fallen yet,' I said, suddenly moved, suddenly quite certain that I sat beside Kipling. 'One day, when there is a new spirit of adventure abroad, we will discover you again.'

'Why have they heaped scorn on me for so long?'

'You were too militant, I suppose—too much of an Empire man. You were too patriotic for your own good.'

He looked a little hurt. 'I was never very political,' he said. 'I wrote over six hundred poems, and you could only call a dozen of them political, I have been abused for harping on the theme of the white man's burden but my only aim was to show off the Empire to my audience—and I believed the Empire was a fine and noble thing. Is it wrong to believe in something? I never went deeply into political issues, that's true. You must remember, my seven years in India were very youthful years. I was in my twenties, a little immature if you like, and my interest in India was a boy's interest. Action appealed to me more than anything else. You must understand that.'

'No one has described action more vividly, or India so well. I feel at one with Kim wherever he goes along the Grand Trunk Road, in the temples at Banaras, amongst the Saharanpur fruit gardens, on the snow-covered Himalaya. Kim has colour and movement and poetry.'

He sighed, and a wistful look came into his eyes.

'I'm prejudiced, of course,' I continued. 'I've spent most of my life in India—not your India, but an India that does still have much of the colour and atmosphere that you captured. You know, Mr Kipling, you can still sit in a third-class railway carriage and meet the most wonderful assortment of people. In any village you will still find the same courtesy, dignity, and courage that the Lama and Kim found on their travels.'

'And the Grand Trunk Road? Is it still a long winding procession of humanity?'

'Well, not exactly,' I said, a little ruefully. 'It's just a procession of motor vehicles now. The poor Lama would be run down by a truck if he became too dreamy on the Grand Trunk Road. Times have changed. There are no more Mrs Hawksbees in Shimla, for instance.'

There was a faraway look in Kipling's eyes. Perhaps

he was imagining himself a boy again; perhaps he could see the hills or the red dust of Rajputana; perhaps he was having a private conversation with Privates Mulvaney and Ortheris, or perhaps he was out hunting with the Seonee wolf-pack. The sound of London's traffic came to us through the glass doors, but we heard only the creaking of bullock cart wheels and the distant music of a flute.

He was talking to himself, repeating a passage from one of his stories.

> And the last puff of the day-wind brought from the unseen villages the scent of damp wood-smoke, hot cakes, dripping undergrowth, and rotting pine-cones. That is the true smell of the Himalayas, and if once it creeps into the blood of a man, that man will at the last, forgetting all else, return to the hills to die.

A mist seemed to have risen between us—or had it come in from the streets?—and when it cleared, Kipling had gone away.

I asked the gatekeeper if he had seen a tall man with a slight stoop, wearing spectacles.

'Nope,' said the gatekeeper. 'Nobody been by for the last ten minutes.'

'Did someone like that come into the gallery a little while ago?'

'No one that I recall. What did you say the bloke's name was?'

'Kipling,' I said.

'Don't know him.'

'Didn't you ever read *The Jungle Book*?'

'Sounds familiar. Tarzan stuff, wasn't it?'

I left the museum, and wandered about the streets for a long time, but I couldn't find Kipling anywhere. Was it the boom of London's traffic that I heard, or the boom of the Sutlej River racing through the valleys?

THE GHOST AND THE IDIOT

In a village near Agra there lived a family who was under the special protection of a munjia, a ghost who lived in a peepul tree. The ghost had attached himself to this particular family and showed his fondness for its members by throwing stones, bones, night soil, and other rubbish at them, and making hideous noises, terrifying them at every opportunity. Under his patronage, the family dwindled away. One by one they died, the only survivor being an idiot boy, whom the ghost did not bother because he felt it beneath his dignity to do so.

But in an Indian village, marriage (like birth and death) must come to all, and it was not long before the neighbours began to make plans for the marriage of the idiot.

The Ghost and the Idiot

After a meeting of the village elders it was decided, first, that the idiot should be married; and second, that he should be married to a shrew of a girl who had passed the age of twenty without finding a suitor!

The shrew and the idiot were soon married off, then left to manage for themselves. The poor idiot had no means of earning a living and had to resort to begging. He had barely been able to support himself before, and now his wife was an additional burden. The first thing she did when she entered the house was to give him a box on the ear and send him out to bring something home for dinner.

The poor fellow went from door to door, but nobody gave him anything, because the same people who had arranged the marriage were annoyed that he had not given them a wedding feast. In the evening, when he returned home empty-handed, his wife cried out: 'Are you back, you lazy idiot? Why have you been so long, and what have you brought for me?' When she found he hadn't even a paisa, she flew into a rage and, removing his head-cloth, tossed it into the peepul tree. Then, taking up her broom, she belaboured her husband until he fled from the house.

But the shrew's anger had not yet been assuaged. Seeing her husband's head-cloth in the peepul tree, she began venting her rage on the tree trunk, accompanying her blows with the most shocking abuse. The ghost who lived in the tree was sensitive to both her blows and her language. Alarmed that her terrible curses might put an end to him, he took to his heels and left the tree in which he had lived for so many years.

Riding on a whirlwind, the ghost soon caught up with the idiot who was still fleeing down the road away from the village. 'Not so fast, brother!' cried the ghost. 'Desert your wife, by all means, but don't abandon your old family ghost! That shrew has driven me out of the peepul tree. What powerful arms she has—and what a vile tongue! She has made brothers of us—brothers in misfortune. And so we must seek our fortunes together! But first promise me you will not return to your wife.'

The idiot made this promise very willingly, and together they journeyed until they reached a large city.

Before they entered the city, the ghost said, 'Now listen, brother. If you follow my advice, your fortune is made. In this city there are two very beautiful girls, one the daughter of the king and the other the daughter of a rich moneylender. I will go and possess the daughter of the king, and when he finds her possessed by a spirit he will try every sort of remedy but with no effect. Meanwhile you must walk daily through the streets in the dress of a sadhu—one who has renounced the world—and when the king comes and asks you if you can cure his daughter, undertake to do so and make your own terms. As soon as I see you, I shall leave the girl. Then I shall go and possess the daughter of the moneylender. But do not go near her, because I am in love with the girl and do not intend giving her up! If you come near her, I shall break your neck.'

The ghost went off on his whirlwind, while the idiot entered the city on his own and found a bed at the local inn for pilgrims. The following day everyone in the city was agog with the news that the king's daughter was dangerously ill. Physicians of all sorts came and went, and all pronounced the girl incurable. The king was on the verge of a nervous breakdown. He offered half his fortune to anyone who could cure his beautiful and only child. The idiot, having smeared himself with dust and ashes like a sadhu, began walking the streets, reciting religious verses.

The people were struck by the idiot's appearance. They took him for a wise and holy man, and reported him to the king, who immediately came into the city, prostrated himself before the idiot, and begged him to cure his daughter. After a show of modesty and reluctance, the idiot was persuaded to accompany the king back to the palace, and the girl was brought before him. Her hair was dishevelled, her teeth were chattering, and her eyes almost starting from their sockets. She howled and cursed and tore at her clothes. The idiot confronted her and recited a few meaningless spells. And the ghost, recognizing him, cried out in terror: 'I'm going, I'm going! I'm on my way!'

'Give me a sign that you have gone,' demanded the idiot.

'As soon as I leave the girl,' said the ghost, 'you will see that mango tree uprooted. That is the sign I'll give.'

A few minutes later the mango tree came crashing down. The girl recovered from her fit and seemed unaware of what had happened. The news of her miraculous cure spread through the city, and the idiot became an object of veneration and wonder. The king kept his word and gave him half his fortune; and so began a period of happiness and prosperity for the idiot.

A few weeks later the ghost took possession of the moneylender's daughter, with whom he was in love. Seeing his daughter take leave of her senses, the moneylender sent for the highly respected idiot and offered him a great sum of money to cure his daughter. But remembering the ghost's warning, the idiot refused. The moneylender was enraged and sent his henchmen to bring the idiot to him by force; and the idiot was dragged along to the rich man's house.

The Ghost and the Idiot

As soon as the ghost saw his old companion, he cried out in a rage: 'Idiot, why have you broken our agreement and come here? Now I will have to break your neck!'

But the idiot, whose reputation for wisdom had actually helped to make him wiser, said, 'Brother ghost I have not come to trouble you but to tell you a terrible piece of news. Old friend and protector, we must leave this city soon. SHE has come here—my dreaded wife!—to torment us both, and to drag us back to the village. She is on her way and will be here any minute!'

When the ghost heard this, he cried out, 'Oh no, oh no! If SHE has come, then we must go!'

And breaking down the walls and doors of the house, the ghost gathered himself up into a little whirlwind and went scurrying out of the city to look for a vacant peepul tree.

The moneylender, delighted that his daughter had been freed of the evil influence, embraced the idiot and showered presents on him. And in due course the idiot married the moneylender's beautiful daughter, inherited his wealth and debtors, and became the richest and most successful moneylender in the city.

THE TROUBLE WITH JINNS

My friend Jimmy has only one arm. He lost the other when he was a young man of twenty-five. The story of how he lost his good right arm is a little difficult to believe, but I swear that it is absolutely true.

To begin with, Jimmy was (and presumably still is) a jinn. Now a jinn isn't really a human like us. A jinn is a spirit creature from another world who has assumed, for a lifetime, the physical aspect of a human being. Jimmy was a true jinn and he had the jinn's gift of being able to elongate his arm at will. Most jinns can stretch their arms to a distance of twenty or thirty feet. Jimmy could attain forty feet. His arm would move through space or up walls or along the ground like a beautiful gliding serpent. I have seen him stretched out beneath a mango tree, helping himself to ripe mangoes from the top of the tree. He loved mangoes. He was a natural glutton and it was probably his gluttony that first led him to misuse his peculiar gifts.

We were at school together at a hill station in northern India. Jimmy was particularly good at basketball. He was clever enough not to lengthen his arm too much because he did not want anyone to know that he was a jinn. In the boxing ring he generally won his fights. His opponents never seemed to get past his amazing reach. He just kept tapping them on the nose until they retired from the ring bloody and bewildered.

It was during the half-term examinations that I stumbled on Jimmy's secret. We had been set a particularly difficult algebra paper but I had managed to cover a couple of sheets with correct answers and was about to forge ahead on another sheet when I noticed someone's hand on my desk. At first I thought it was the invigilator's. But when I looked up there was no one beside me.

Could it be the boy sitting directly behind? No, he was engrossed in his question paper and had his hands to himself. Meanwhile, the hand on my desk had grasped my answer sheets and was cautiously moving off. Following its descent, I found that it was attached to an arm of amazing length and pliability. It moved stealthily down the desk and slithered across the floor, shrinking all the while, until it was restored to its normal length. Its owner was of course one who had never been any good at algebra.

I had to write out my answers a second time but after the exam I went straight up to Jimmy, told him I didn't like his game and threatened to expose him. He begged me not to let anyone know, assured me that he couldn't really help himself, and offered to be of service to me whenever I wished. It was tempting to have Jimmy as my friend, for with his long reach he would obviously be useful. I agreed to overlook the matter of the pilfered papers and we became the best of pals.

It did not take me long to discover that Jimmy's gift was more of a nuisance than a constructive aid. That was because Jimmy had a second-rate mind and did not know how to make proper use of his powers. He seldom rose above the trivial. He used his long arm in the tuck shop, in the classroom, in the dormitory. And when we were allowed out to the cinema, he used it in the dark of the hall.

Now the trouble with all jinns is that they have a weakness for women with long black hair. The longer and blacker the hair, the better for jinns. And should a jinn manage to take possession of the woman he desires, she goes into a decline and her beauty decays. Everything about her is destroyed except for the beautiful long black hair.

Jimmy was still too young to be able to take possession in this way, but he couldn't resist touching and stroking long black hair. The cinema was the best place for the indulgence of his whims. His arm would start stretching, his fingers would feel their way along the rows of seats, and his lengthening limb would slowly work its way along the aisle until it reached the back of the seat in which sat the object of his admiration. His hand would stroke the long black hair with great tenderness and if the girl felt anything and looked around, Jimmy's hand would disappear behind the seat and lie there poised like the hood of a snake, ready to strike again.

At college, two or three years later, Jimmy's first real victim succumbed to his attentions. She was a lecturer in economics, not very good-looking, but her hair, black and lustrous, reached almost to her knees. She usually kept it in plaits but Jimmy saw her one morning just after she had taken a head bath, and her hair lay spread out on the cot on which she was reclining. Jimmy could no longer control himself. His spirit, the very essence of his personality, entered the woman's body and the next day, she was distraught, feverish, and excited. She would not eat, went into a coma, and in a few days, dwindled to a mere skeleton. When she died, she was nothing but

The Shadow on the Wall

skin and bone but her hair had lost none of its loveliness.

I took pains to avoid Jimmy after this tragic event. I could not prove that he was the cause of the lady's sad demise but in my own heart I was quite certain of it. For since meeting Jimmy, I had read a good deal about jinns and knew their ways.

We did not see each other for a few years. And then, holidaying in the hills last year, I found we were staying at the same hotel. I could not very well ignore him and after we had drunk a few beers together I began to feel that I had perhaps misjudged Jimmy and that he was not the irresponsible jinn I had taken him for. Perhaps the college lecturer had died of some mysterious malady that attacks only college lecturers and Jimmy had nothing at all to do with it.

We had decided to take our lunch and a few bottles of beer to a grassy knoll just below the main motor road. It was late afternoon and I had been sleeping off the effects of the beer when I woke up to find Jimmy looking rather agitated.

'What's wrong?' I asked.

'Up there, under the pine trees,' he said. 'Just above the road. Don't you see them?'

'I see two girls,' I said. 'So what?'

'The one on the left. Haven't you noticed her hair?'

'Yes, it is very long and beautiful and—now look, Jimmy, you'd better get a grip on yourself!' But already his hand was out of sight, his arm snaking up the hillside and across the road.

Presently, I saw the hand emerge from some bushes near the girls and then cautiously make its way to the girl with the black tresses. So absorbed was Jimmy in the pursuit of his favourite pastime that he failed to hear the blowing of a horn. Around the bend of the road came a speeding Mercedes-Benz truck.

Jimmy saw the truck but there wasn't time for him to shrink his arm back to normal. It lay right across the entire width of the road and when the truck had passed over it, it writhed and twisted like a mortally wounded python.

By the time the truck driver and I could fetch a doctor, the arm (or what was left of it) had shrunk to its ordinary size. We took Jimmy to hospital where the doctors found it necessary to amputate. The truck driver, who kept insisting that the arm he ran over was at least thirty feet long, was arrested on a charge of drunken driving.

Some weeks later, I asked Jimmy, 'Why are you so depressed? You still have one arm. Isn't it gifted in the same way?'

'I never tried to find out,' he said, 'and I'm not going to try now.'

He is, of course, still a jinn at heart and whenever he sees a girl with long black hair he must be terribly tempted to try out his one good arm and stroke her beautiful tresses. But he has learnt his lesson. It is better to be a human without any gifts than a jinn or a genius with one too many.

WILSON'S BRIDGE

The old wooden bridge has gone, and today an iron suspension bridge straddles the Bhagirathi as it rushes down the gorge below the Gangotri. But villagers will tell you that you can still hear the hooves of Wilson's horse as he gallops across the bridge he had built 150 years ago. At the time people were sceptical of its safety, and so, to prove its sturdiness, he rode across it again and again. Parts of the old bridge can still be seen on the far bank of the river. And the legend of Wilson and his pretty hill bride, Gulabi, is still well-known in this region.

I had joined some friends in the old forest rest house near the river. There were the Rays, recently married, and the Duttas, married many years. The younger Rays quarrelled frequently; the older Duttas looked on with more amusement than concern. I was a part of their group and yet something of an outsider. As a single man, I was a person of no importance. And as a marriage counsellor, I wouldn't have been of any use to them.

I spent most of my time wandering along the riverbanks or exploring the thick deodar and oak forests that covered the slopes. It was these trees that had made a fortune for Wilson and his patron, the Raja of Tehri. They had exploited the great forests to the full, floating huge logs downstream to the timber yards in the plains.

Returning to the rest house late one evening, I was halfway across the bridge when I saw a figure at the other end, emerging from the mist. Presently I made out a woman, wearing the plain dhoti of the hills; her hair fell loose over her shoulders. She appeared not to see me, and reclined against the railing of the bridge, looking down at the rushing waters far below. And then, to my amazement and horror, she climbed over the railing and threw herself into the river.

I ran forward, calling out, but I reached the railing only to see her fall into the foaming waters below, from where she was carried swiftly downstream.

The watchman's cabin stood a little way off. The door was open. The watchman, Ram Singh, was reclining on his bed, smoking a hookah.

'Someone just jumped off the bridge,' I said breathlessly. 'She's been swept down the river!'

The watchman was unperturbed. 'Gulabi again,' he said, almost to himself; and then to me, 'Did you see her clearly?'

'Yes, a woman with long loose hair—but I didn't see her face very clearly.'

'It must have been Gulabi. Only a ghost, my dear sir. Nothing to be alarmed about. Every now and then someone sees her throw herself into the river. Sit down,' he said, gesturing towards a battered old armchair, 'be comfortable and I'll tell you all about it.'

I was far from comfortable, but I listened to Ram Singh tell me the tale of Gulabi's suicide. After making me a glass of hot sweet tea, he launched into a long, rambling account of how Wilson, a British adventurer seeking his fortune, had been hunting musk deer when he encountered Gulabi on the path from her village. The girl's grey-green eyes and peach-blossom complexion enchanted him, and he went out of his way to get to know her people. Was he in love with her, or did he simply find her beautiful and desirable? We shall never really know. In the course of his travels and adventures he had known many women, but Gulabi was different, childlike and ingenuous, and he decided he would marry her. The humble family to which she belonged had no objection. Hunting had its limitations, and Wilson found it more profitable to tap the region's great forest wealth. In a few years he had made a fortune. He built a large timbered house at Harsil, another in Dehradun, and a third at Mussoorie. Gulabi had all she could have wanted, including two robust little sons. When he was away on work, she looked after their children and their large apple orchard at Harsil.

And then came the evil day when Wilson met the Englishwoman, Ruth, on the Mussoorie Mall, and decided that she should have a share of his affections and his wealth. A fine house was provided for her, too. The time he spent at Harsil with Gulabi and his children dwindled. 'Business affairs'—he was now one of the owners of a bank—kept him in the fashionable hill resort. He was a popular host and took his friends and associates on shikar parties in the Doon.

Gulabi brought up her children in village style. She heard stories of Wilson's dalliance with the Mussoorie woman and, on one of his rare visits, she confronted him and voiced her resentment, demanding that he leave the other woman. He brushed her aside and told her not to listen to idle gossip. When he turned away from her, she picked up the flintlock pistol that lay on the gun table and fired one shot at him. The bullet missed him and shattered her looking glass. Gulabi ran out of the house, through the orchard and into the forest, then down the steep path to the bridge built by Wilson only two or three years before. When he had recovered his composure, he mounted his horse and came looking for her. It was too late. She had already thrown herself off the bridge into the swirling waters far below. Her body was found a mile or two downstream, caught between some rocks.

This was the tale that Ram Singh told me, with various flourishes and interpolations of his own. I thought it would make a good story to tell my friends that evening, before the fireside in the rest house. They found the story fascinating, but when I told them I had seen Gulabi's ghost, they thought I was doing a little embroidering of my own. Mrs Dutta thought it was a tragic tale. Young Mrs Ray thought Gulabi had been very silly. 'She was a simple girl,' opined Mr Dutta. 'She responded in the only way she knew…'; 'Money can't buy happiness,' said Mr Ray. 'No,' said Mrs Dutta, 'but it can buy you a great many comforts.' Mrs Ray wanted to talk of other things, so I changed the subject. It can get a little confusing for a bachelor who must spend the evening with two married couples. There are undercurrents which he is aware of but not equipped to deal with.

The Shadow on the Wall

I would walk across the bridge quite often after that. It was busy with traffic during the day, but after dusk there were only a few vehicles on the road and seldom any pedestrians. A mist rose from the gorge below and obscured the far end of the bridge. I preferred walking there in the evening, half-expecting, half-hoping to see Gulabi's ghost again. It was her face that I really wanted to see. Would she still be as beautiful as she was fabled to be?

It was on the evening before our departure that something happened that would haunt me for a long time afterwards.

There was a feeling of restiveness as our days there drew to a close. The Rays had apparently made up their differences, although they weren't talking very much. Mr Dutta was anxious to get back to his office in Delhi and Mrs Dutta's rheumatism was playing up. I was restless too, wanting to return to my writing desk in Mussoorie.

That evening I decided to take one last stroll across the bridge to enjoy the cool breeze of a summer's night in the mountains. The moon hadn't come up, and it was really quite dark, although there were lamps at either end of the bridge providing sufficient light for those who wished to cross over.

I was standing in the middle of the bridge, in the

darkest part, listening to the river thundering down the gorge, when I saw the sari-draped figure emerging from the lamplight and making towards the railings.

Instinctively I called out, 'Gulabi!'

She half-turned towards me, but I could not see her clearly. The wind had blown her hair across her face and all I saw was wildly staring eyes. She raised herself over the railing and threw herself off the bridge. I heard the splash as her body struck the water far below.

Once again I found myself running towards the part of the railing where she had jumped. And then someone was running towards the same spot, from the direction of the rest house. It was young Mr Ray.

'My wife!' he cried out. 'Did you see my wife?'

He rushed to the railing and stared down at the swirling waters of the river.

'Look! There she is!' He pointed at a helpless figure bobbing about in the water.

We ran down the steep bank to the river but the current had swept her on. Scrambling over rocks and bushes, we made frantic efforts to catch up with the drowning woman. But the river in that defile is a roaring torrent, and it was over an hour before we were able to retrieve poor Mrs Ray's body, caught in driftwood about a mile downstream.

She was cremated not far from where we found her and we returned to our various homes in gloom and grief, chastened but none the wiser for the experience.

If you happen to be in that area and decide to cross the bridge late in the evening, you might see Gulabi's ghost or hear the hoof beats of Wilson's horse as he canters across the old wooden bridge looking for her. Or you might see the ghost of Mrs Ray and hear her husband's anguished cry. Or there might be others. Who knows?

A FACE UNDER THE PILLOW

'Camping in the jungle was full of danger,' I remarked. 'You must have felt much safer working in the house.'

'Well, cooking was certainly easier,' said Mehmood. 'But I don't know if it was much safer. The animals couldn't get in, true, but there were ghosts and evil spirits lurking in some of the rooms. I changed my room thrice, but there was always someone—something—after me. I don't know if I should tell you this, baba. You have your own small room and you may start imagining things...'

'I'm not afraid of ghosts, Mehmood.'

'That's because you haven't seen one. Although I'm not sure it was a ghost. And I did not actually see anything. But I felt it all right!'

'You can't feel a ghost, Mehmood. At least not in stories.'

'This wasn't a story. It was my first night in Carpet-sahib's house in the jungle. It has a big house with many rooms, and I was given a room of my own. But there was no electricity in that out-of-the-way place. We used kerosene lamps or candles.

'I had brought my own razai and blanket, but the mattress was a strange one, and so was the pillow. Not a pillow, really, but an old cushion, very hard and lumpy. It was my first night in that bed, and I was very uncomfortable. The candle burnt itself out, and I was still wide awake. I could see very little, there was just a small window allowing a little moonlight into the room. I was almost asleep when I heard someone groaning beside me. Groaning loudly, as though in pain. But there was no one else in the bed, and no one beneath it.

'The groaning stopped for a time, and then, just as I was about to fall asleep, it started again. Groan, groan, groan. Now it seemed to come from beneath my pillow.

'I turned on my side, and slowly, carefully, I slipped my hand beneath the pillow.

'It encountered a hairy face, a gaping mouth, hollow sockets instead of eyes. Horrible to touch! Not the face of a human, baba—the face of a rakshas!

A Face Under the Pillow

'I tried to pull my hand away, but it was seized by that terrible mouth. A mouth with long sharp teeth—teeth like daggers! It would have bitten my fingers off if I hadn't screamed and shouted for help.

'Carpet-sahib and his sister and the other servants came running. As they rushed into the room with torches and a lamp, these awful teeth released my hand.

'Under the pillow!' I screamed. 'Under the pillow!'

'They looked under the pillow! But there was nothing there. I showed them my fingers—they were bleeding badly.'

'A rat must have bitten you,' said Carpet-sahib's sister. But she knew it wasn't a rat. And she gave me another room to sleep in.

'And were you all right in the second room?'

'For a couple of nights, baba. And then it happened again.'

'You put your hand under the pillow again? And the face was there?'

'Not the whole face, baba. Just something soft and squishy. I thought it was a snail under my pillow. So I got up, lit my lamp, and looked under the pillow.'

'What was it, Mehmood? Tell me quickly.'

'It was an eyeball, baba. An eye that had been removed from its socket. It was staring up at me. Just an eyeball, staring! I picked it up and threw it out of the window. I threw the pillow away too. Something terrible had happened upon that pillow, I'm sure of it.'

'So it wasn't the room?'

'It wasn't the room. It was the pillow, baba. Next day I went into town and bought a new pillow, and from then on I slept beautifully every night. Never use a strange cushion or pillow, baba. Terrible things have happened on pillows. So remember—when you return to school next month, take a new pillow, and don't use anyone else's!'

After listening to Mehmood's story, I was always careful to use my own pillow. Even now, many, many years later, I carry my own pillow wherever I go. No hotel pillows for me. You never knew what might be lurking beneath them.

HAUNTED PLACES

THE ROCKING CHAIR
Yes, sometimes old houses do give you a feeling of still being occupied by the ghosts or spirits of long-dead occupants—people who once lived and loved beneath that weathered roof and between those listening walls.

The walls listen to us by day; and when, late at night, the residents are asleep, they and the rest of the house come to life, gossip among themselves, and discuss the strengths and weaknesses of the human guests. Those walls, those pictures, those old tables and armchairs have seen triumph and tragedy, and sometimes they resonate with these things and release some of what they have absorbed.

Like that old rocking chair I picked up in the antique

shop near Landour's clock tower. I had no desire to purchase or own a rocking chair, but when I spotted it in a corner of the shop I couldn't resist sitting down in it; and finding that it suited my ample proportions I remained seated for some time, becoming increasingly aware that I belonged to it in some way and that I ought to possess it.

We haggled over the price, and I ended up paying more than it seemed to be worth, although the shop owner maintained that it had once belonged to a royal family. A Nepali labourer carried it on his back and delivered it to my rooms higher up the hillside, and I found a place for it in a corner of my sunny bedroom.

Every afternoon I would settle into that rocking chair, read a little, and then rock myself to sleep until Beena woke me up with a cup of tea. I had the rocking chair all to myself—by day, that is…

It was only at night, late at night, that someone else seemed to occupy it.

The chair had been in my room for a few days, getting used to its new surroundings I suppose. Then, one night, I was woken by a rhythmical creaking sound, and switching on the bed light I saw that the rocking chair was in motion, oscillating back and forth as though it had an occupant.

Well, there was no one in it, and I came to the conclusion that it had been set in motion by the light breeze from my open window, kept open on summer nights.

This happened on several occasions and I was getting quite used to it when, late one night, the rocking was more rapid and vigorous than usual, and I turned on the light to see a tiny old woman sitting in the chair, rocking to and fro, and grinning at me in a rather childish manner. There were rings on her fingers and she appeared to be dressed in an expensive gown. But she had no teeth, and this gave a sort of malevolent leer to her grin.

I shot out of bed, and as I did so the figure of the old woman vanished. The empty chair kept rocking.

Next day I removed it to the attic. If the ghost of old ladies wanted to use it, they were welcome to do so, but not in my bedroom. And when I spoke to the antique shop owner about this vision of mine, he confessed that the rocking chair had once belonged to the Rani of —, and that she had died in it, at an advanced age.

The rocking chair is still in my attic. I don't go up there at night. But the other day, while reading in my little sunroom, I heard the creaking of the chair and felt bold enough to climb the stairs to see if it had a visitor.

It was only the neighbourhood cat, a large tabby,

curled up in the middle of the chair, enjoying its motion.

Perhaps the old rani likes having a little company, because the cat is there quite often, purring contentedly, while an unseen hand strokes it behind the ears. I don't disturb them. Cats see more than we do. And if the rocking chair can give pleasure to the ghost of an old rani, she's more than welcome to it.

But I don't go up to the attic at night. I might just see her again.

A HAUNTED HOUSE

Back in the 1950's, when I was still in my teens, I would often wander up the Rajpur Road, a quiet tree-lined highway with a few old bungalows scattered here and there. One of them, a two-storeyed building, had lain empty and abandoned for several years. It was reputed to be haunted, and no one was interested in buying or renting it. Even passers-by gave it a wide berth.

I had seen the house from outside, but I had never ventured into its grounds. The story of the haunting, if indeed it was a haunting, went like this: An elderly English couple, childless, had owned the house and lived in it for many years. But when they grew old their income from investments dwindled, and at the time of Independence they were really hard up. Being old and reclusive, they had been forgotten by the rest of the community, most of whom were busy making arrangements to leave the country. By the end of 1948 most of the Anglo-Indians and Europeans in Dehra had left for 'home' (the U. K.) but the old couple had stayed on, more from compulsion than desire. They had, indeed, been quite forgotten—until, one day, a bill collector (for light or water or some unpaid services) entered the house and found the old couple dead in their large four-poster bed. They had died of starvation, probably within a few hours of each other. The post-mortem revealed that their stomachs were empty.

It was a sad story and a depressing one, and people did not want to talk about it. It was nobody's fault, but we all feel a little guilty when a fellow human dies of neglect.

I was curious about the deserted house but I was afraid to enter it on my own. Instead I wandered about the grounds, a wilderness of overgrown shrubs and dying rose bushes. Here and there a flowering plant had struggled to survive but tall grasses and weeds were taking over.

As I was about to leave from the broken gate, I was hailed by my cousin Ronald, who was passing by on his bicycle.

'Hey, Ruskin, what are you doing there? Have you become a ghost-hunter now?'

'Just looking around,' I said, feeling a bit foolish. Did I really expect to see a couple of ghosts?

'I'll come and join you,' said Ronald. 'But first let me fetch some grub. You can't look for ghosts on an empty stomach.' And off he rode, in the direction of the Ellora Bakery.

He was an impulsive fellow, and I wasn't sure if he'd come back; but twenty minutes later he came cycling through the open gate, his shopping basket topped up with pastries, buns, cheese rolls, chicken patties, sandwiches.... Ronald's pocket money far exceeded mine. His father owned a cinema; my stepfather owed money all over the town.

'Let's go inside,' said Ronald. 'It's hot out here. And ghosts don't sunbathe.'

So far I'd remained in the garden, reluctant to venture into the house on my own. But Ronald showed no compunction about going in; I simply followed.

Most of the furniture had gone from the rooms. In the hall was a sofa with the stuffing exposed; in the dining room a table and a couple of broken chairs; in the bedroom a large double-bed without any mattress or coverings. Anything that could be sold had been taken away, probably by vandals.

We weren't vandals, but we were a couple of ghouls, picnicking in the ruined home of people who had died in tragic circumstances. But Ronald was very blasé about the whole thing. For him it was enormous fun.

'Tuck in, Ruskin,' he said, spreading out all the delicacies on a dressing table, its mirror broken. 'They must have looked in it every day, except towards the end.'

I was beginning to lose my appetite. Those old people had starved to death, and here we were, glutting ourselves on cakes and savouries. When I commented on this fact, Ronald said, 'Pooh! It wasn't our fault, what happened. They're welcome to join us, if they are still around.'

But no one was around. A haunted house? The rooms were entirely without any atmosphere. Just dust everywhere, and cobwebs.

A large spider ran across the bed.

'We'll leave a pastry for the spider,' said Ronald. 'And since you're not eating anything, we'll leave the rest for the old folk.'

'Don't leave any food here,' I said. 'It seems rather—'
'What?'
'Well, disrespectful.'
'You are an old-fashioned fellow, Ruskin. Come on, let's go. I want to catch the matinee at three. They're

showing *Ben-Hur* at the Odeon.'

I walked with him to the gate. No, I had no premonition of disaster, but I declined his invitation to take a ride on his pillion, and as for *Ben-Hur*, those quasi-Biblical spectacles, with their 'casts of millions', failed to excite me.

Ronald hopped on to his bicycle and, as was his habit, rode off at speed as though he were in a cycle race. Always up to new tricks, he grabbed the fender of a small truck and allowed it to carry him some distance. As it picked up speed, he let go and swerved into the centre of the road. At the same time an army truck, coming from the opposite direction, slammed straight into the cyclist, sending him sprawling and then running over the helpless boy.

It all happened very suddenly. I stood there, petrified. People ran to Ronald's aid, and within minutes the truck driver and his mates had taken the badly injured boy to the army hospital in the nearby cantonment. But Ronald did not survive the impact of the collision. It was no one's fault, just the logical outcome of his reckless nature.

And we hadn't seen any ghosts. But had they seen us? Do we see the stars at noon? They are there all the same, looking down at us, and it is we who cannot see them.

Ronald's parents were devastated by the tragedy, for

he had been their only son. I had never been very close to him, but I had seen the accident and it scarred my memories for many years. It helped to convince me that life is not about rewards and punishments, but about consequences.

∫

A HAUNTED PLANET

There is no ghost more dangerous or intractable than the Covid virus that has infiltrated the human race in the course of the last two years. Invisible! Unstoppable! Everywhere at once. Baffling and teasing scientists, rendering the gurus and godmen bereft of platitudes, bringing out the best in some of us, the worst in others.

A true ghost, travelling the globe without passport, without hindrance. Happiest in a crowd, moving unseen amongst the revellers or protestors or worshippers, regardless of what brings people together. A lover of crowds, this ghost, but it will follow you to a distant village or lonely hilltop if it so wishes.

Is it nature in revolt, now telling us that we are not the masters after all, and that there is a limit to how much we can destroy and poison and desiccate this unique planet...who knows?

Perhaps the haunting will subside and we will know then. Or is it too late to learn from our follies?

∽

2 A.M.

Two o'clock in the morning—the darkest hour, when our energy, mental and physical, is at its lowest. For those who are critically ill, the tide is running out. For those who cannot sleep it is a dead, depressing hour.

Because of a prostate problem I have to get up at least three times in the night to ease the pressure on my bladder. Twelve o'clock or thereabouts; at about 2 a.m.; and then at about four in the morning. At twelve o'clock there are some who are still awake. At four in the morning there are some who are getting up because they have a busy day ahead—a plane to catch or a long road journey. But at two or three in the morning nobody's about. The silence is deafening. Even the dogs have stopped barking; the neighbourhood dogs who bark simply because other dogs are barking.

And then, the other night, something unusual

happened. I had just returned from the bathroom and was about to hop into bed when I heard a loud knocking on the front door.

A visitor at 2 a.m.? I couldn't think of anyone who would want to drop in for a chat in the dead of night. It had to be an emergency. I put on my dressing-gown, went to the front door and opened it without hesitation.

Standing there, about nine or ten feet tall, was a woman in black, towering over me. It could have been a man, but I had the impression it was a woman, possibly a nun, because she was dressed in black from head to foot. I couldn't see her face, but I saw her hands—large hands with long scabrous fingers.

I had the fright of my life. This was Death's Dark Angel, if ever there was one. I tried to close the door, but she had slipped that questing hand between the doors and was pushing against them. In desperation I caught one of her fingers and bent it backwards, and finally she drew her hand away and I was able to shut and bolt the door.

I returned to my bedroom, unsure if I was enacting a dream or experiencing something very tangible and real. I sat on the edge of my bed, knowing I wouldn't be able to sleep. I turned off the light. And then, just as I did so, the knocking started again. But this time it was at the window. Someone was standing on the window-ledge, two storeys above the road, tapping on the windowpanes.

The curtains were drawn. I made a dash for them, pulled them aside, and opened the window. Opened it wide. This was an impulsive act, not a brave one. But I felt I had to confront this awful visitor.

There was no one there. She had made her presence felt, and then she had gone.

2 a.m.

The dead of night. When the dead still roam.